A STREAK OF BAD CLUCK

ELLEN RIGGS

BOUGHT-THE-FARM
MYSTERIES

FREE PREQUEL

Rescuing this pup could bring Ivy a whole new life... if it doesn't kill her first.

Discover how big city executive Ivy meets Keats, her crime-solving sheepdog, in A Dog with Two Tales. This short prequel to the laugh-out-loud Bought-the-Farm Mystery series is a page-turner for lovers of animals, humor and spunky amateur sleuths. Join Ellen Riggs' author newsletter at **ellenriggs.com/opt-in** and get this BONUS novella.

A Streak of Bad Cluck

Copyright © 2020 Ellen Riggs

ISBN 978-1-989303-51-1 eBook
ISBN 978-1-989303-52-8 Book
ASIN B0859PBQZL Kindle
ASIN 1989303528 Paperback

Publisher: Ellen Riggs
www.ellenriggs.com
Cover designer: Lou Harper
Editor: Serena Clarke
2211172144

CHAPTER ONE

The white tuft on Keats' tail fanned as he trotted ahead of me to the barn. He'd already been awake for an hour, sitting beside my bed in the darkness and *willing* me to get the day started. Since our move from the city to Runaway Farm, the dog's switch was permanently stuck in the "on" position. There was always something a brilliant, busybody border collie needed to be doing, and it all started with staring me awake before dawn. Sometimes I wondered if he could see into my dreams, because he frequently interrupted nightmares that continued to haunt me. As grateful as I was to leave those behind, most days I was as tired as Keats was energized. Corporate life hadn't prepared me for all this activity.

By the time we got this far, Aladdin, the resident rooster, had typically declared the day officially open for business. Today we beat him. That was a small miracle, surpassed only by the miracle trailing after me in pink floral pajamas. Jilly Blackwood, my best friend, almost never entered the barn or henhouse and she wasn't a morning person. I could only assume she was worried about me, after my recent brush with death. Make that brushes with deaths. Plural. I wanted to tell her that I was coping just fine but that would only convince her I was in complete denial. It wasn't denial. I'd been through a lot, but my years as an HR exec had taught me how to compartmentalize. The compartment containing the trauma mainly opened at night to release nasty little demons into my dreams.

"You didn't need to come," I said, as Jilly yawned audibly. Our breath streamed out into the chilly late October air. Aside from Keats' patches of pristine white fur, not much else was visible in the dim light. "I've got the egg run covered."

"Keats thought otherwise," she said. "He scratched my door to wake me up."

"Really? Keats, that was rude and unnecessary."

The dog turned and his eerie blue eye winked. He liked to run a tight ship and today he wanted all hands on deck.

"He's just looking out for us," Jilly said. "I'm anxious about the new guests arriving and I'm sure he is, too. Aren't you, Ivy?"

"I'd be a fool not to be." I veered to the right and then circled the barn. The henhouse was on the far side, where the conditions were perfect for a flock of nearly 40. I couldn't take credit for knowing that. I'd bought this hobby farm and inn for a song from Hannah Pemberton, the heiress who'd owned and loved it dearly before me. When she got called away to run her family's business in Europe, she'd chosen me to take over based on my rather dramatic rescue of the know-it-all sheepdog prancing ahead of us. "Our first guests were a nightmare and this group won't be much better."

"Well, they couldn't be worse," Jilly said. "Seriously. It's highly unlikely that anyone in the Clover Grove Bridge Club will murder someone during a weekend stay."

I sighed. "You wouldn't think so. But I wouldn't have thought it possible that Runaway Farm would see two murders in barely two months."

"True." Jilly puffed a little as she tried to keep up. I knew the path better and was also picking up speed with the discussion of murder. "The Bridge Buddies have been around forever, right? If they were going to kill each other, they'd have done it by now."

"I'm sure they've been tempted," I said. "From what I hear, each member has something on the others. That's how they maintain the balance of power."

"Lovely," Jilly said. "Sounds like the relaxing vibe we want at the inn."

Reaching the door to the henhouse, I turned and smiled. "Maybe we've been doing friendship all wrong, Jilly. The Bridge Biddies have staying power."

"Bridge Biddies! Did you make that up?"

"All credit to my mom," I said. "She's still bitter after they drove her out of her favorite hair salon. I'll let her share the sordid tale when you're swapping beauty tips. In case you haven't noticed, you've become her favorite daughter. Which is saying something when she has five."

"Your mom's a hoot," Jilly said, laughing. "I like her."

My mom, Dahlia Galloway, was most certainly that. In a town filled to the brim with eccentrics, she was known as "a real character." That took effort.

The sudden hoot of a barn owl made us jump and turn. It was already a little brighter and I could see the dusty gravel driveway unfurling beyond us. The distant crunching of footsteps reached my ears.

Standing on tiptoe, I squinted. "Who is that?" I watched a figure pick up speed to reach the turnoff to the trail that ran between all the neighboring properties. It was like a bush highway, generally used on four-wheelers or a tractor. "I recognize that gait, although she's really hoofing it. It's Edna Evans."

"Why on earth is an eighty-year-old wandering around out here before first light?" Jilly asked. "It's not safe. She could fall."

"She's probably got her broom for easy takeoff." Edna, my

nearest neighbor, was a retired nurse with a sadistic streak who enjoyed playing me like a fish on a line. It worked, too, despite my excellent HR skills. I knew how to manage people, and since I couldn't manage Edna, I could only conclude that she wasn't human.

"Get the jokes out of your system now, so you can keep a straight face later," Jilly said. "Maybe Edna was doing an inspection before her bridge buddies arrive. Since she recommended holding their tournament here, she probably feels her reputation is on the line."

"Let's hear it from the witch's mouth," I said, walking to the driveway. "Edna! EDNA!"

She turned to glance in our direction and then plunged abruptly into the bushes. Even in autumn, the vegetation was dense and thorny, but Edna knew the terrain well. My brother Asher, a police officer known for liking everyone *except* Edna Evans, said she'd been fined by the County half a dozen times for illegal wildlife snares. Regardless, she wore her rabbit fur wrap and accessories with a nonchalance I envied.

There was a strange noise near my feet. Keats had probably been trying to catch my eye, and failing that, offered his opinion aloud in his odd mumble-talk. Looking down, I saw his ruff was up and his tail was down. That was strange. Not the mumble-talking—he did that all the time—but he didn't normally waste his hackles on Edna Evans. We were at her house every day delivering the fresh eggs and gourmet food she'd extorted from me before sharing information about the most recent murder, of my former boss from Flordale Corporation.

"Keats seems spooked," Jilly said. Her green eyes now shone in the bright slash of sunlight creeping over the horizon. "Maybe it wasn't Edna."

"Pretty sure it was. She has a bit of a limp," I said, shrugging as I turned back. "Well, it's not worth following when I need to pick her up in a few hours anyway. I bet you're right that she was making sure the grounds were up to her standards."

Edna was a Bridge Buddy in good standing, but her reputation had suffered after the murder of Lloyd Boyce, the local dogcatcher, on Runaway Farm the week I arrived. Edna had been caught spying and failing to report information to the authorities. She'd pretty much flipped her rabbit accessories at police chief Kellan Harper, but she actually cared about her cronies' opinion. So now she was trying to get back in their good graces by helping to host a weekend bridge tournament at my inn. The ladies, all seniors, lived in or around town but staying here meant they'd get waited on hand and foot, and would only need to leave their game for bathroom breaks.

"Let's hurry and get back to the house," Jilly said. "Keats is spooking me, now."

We'd both learned to trust Keats' reaction to humans and animals alike. He had uncanny powers of observation that were typical of his breed, but sometimes it felt like he had an intuition that went far beyond any dog's. He certainly sensed my intentions even before I knew what I wanted. If he didn't approve of my plans, he had no problem telling me so, either in his own mumbled language, or by literally herding me where he thought I should go. I wasn't the alpha leader I should be, but we made a great team.

"It's hard not to be spooked around here these days," I said. "But what could be less threatening than a henhouse?"

I reached for the latch on the door and my hand stopped in mid-air. It was unfastened and the door was slightly ajar. The night before, I'd checked the doors at last call, like I always did.

"Do you think Edna was inside?" Jilly said.

"Looks like it. Since I deliver her eggs, I assume she wanted to visit her hens. I guess they were more like pets than she let on."

A few weeks earlier, Edna had demanded I shut down her own small coop and collect her hens. She'd said the upkeep was too much at her age, although she got around like a woman decades younger.

"This day is getting weird even before it officially starts," Jilly said.

At that moment, Aladdin unleashed his proud crow at close range, making us jump again.

"*Now* it's official," I said. "I'll ask Charlie to put a lock on this door today. Edna is welcome to come over in proper visiting hours but I don't need her creeping around at night and then suing me when she breaks a limb."

Inside, I switched on the light and we both let out a long sigh. There was something instantly calming about a chicken coop, which is probably why they'd become so popular in Clover Grove. When I left for college, the town was moving away from its agricultural roots, but homesteaders had claimed it in recent years, and the place was all about fresh eggs, goat cheese and soap, and preserved "heritage" vegetables and fruit. Part of me still wanted to roll my eyes, but I was living in a glass house. In fact, I was blessed to live in a glorious renovated farmhouse and inn that exploited guests' desires to get back to the land for a short time.

I scanned to see if anything looked amiss, but Keats' ruff had settled and the hens themselves were calm, so I figured all was well. My eyes landed on Edna's favorite hen, a white silky bantam named Sookie. Edna had insisted on delivering Sookie's nest box herself, and putting it on a high shelf. Although most of the hens shuffled their spots, Sookie returned to her personal palace every night and left an egg there every morning. I never saw Sookie fight for her spot, although there was many a dustup among the feathered gals for less.

"Edna must adore Sookie if she's visiting at the crack of dawn," Jilly said, dropping a casual egg pun into the conversation with a grin. "I guess she's not all bad."

"Oh, she's all bad. If she can hike through the bush in the dark, why have I suddenly become her handmaid, delivering food and picking her up on command?"

"She even dictated the menu." Jilly frowned at that. She was on leave from her corporate headhunting firm in Boston to run the kitchen at Runaway Inn and didn't take kindly to being told what to serve. "Right down to monogrammed crème brûlée for dinner tonight."

"I guess she wants to showcase her eggs," I said, handing Jilly a basket before starting to collect the coop's spoils.

"Everyone had special requests," Jilly said. "One hates cucumber and another red pepper. One can't eat chicken, and another beef. And none of them can digest legumes. It's going to be a tough group, Ivy. I'm beginning to wonder if they all will be."

"Regretting your career change?" I asked, slipping my hand into each nest and gently pulling out eggs. There was something so satisfying about finding a perfect egg under a hen. Perhaps it was childhood memories of Easter, although with five siblings and little money, holiday treats were few and far between.

"Not for a second," Jilly said. "Despite our misadventures. But I look forward to when you can be more choosy about who you accept into the inn."

"Me too." The two murders had left me feeling a little desperate to drum up business. "At least we'll get more hosting practice."

My phone rang and I pulled it out of the front pocket of my bibbed overalls with my free hand. "It's Edna," I said, checking the display. "How did she get home so fast? She doesn't have a cell, although she should if she's going to traipse in the bush."

"Do not let her get to you," Jilly said. "We have superb people skills, remember? Let's dig deep and channel them this weekend."

"A tall order, my friend." I pressed talk and then speaker. "Morning, Miss Evans. Why were you—"

"I don't have time for chitchat, Ivy." Edna's voice rang out in the henhouse and Sookie immediately fluttered from her nest to a perch beside me, as if wanting to get closer to her former owner. "This is the event of a lifetime. I hope you're ready for it."

"We are. Sookie says hi, by the way. She wants to know—"

"I don't talk to animals like they're babies, Ivy Galloway. You're far too attached to these chickens and it's going to bite you in the behind one of these days."

"Peck," I said. "Chickens don't have teeth."

"They can certainly deliver a bite you'll remember." There was a loud sigh at the other end. "Do you really have time to debate when the bridge ladies will be there in a few hours? It's going to be intense, Ivy. You need to bring your A game."

"Which reminds me," I said. "Why aren't you playing in the tourney, Miss Evans?"

"So I can watch over you and that giddy friend of yours. She may be a good cook but your brother could do so much better than a city girl with small town affectations."

Jilly opened her mouth but I raised a finger. "Edna, please be respectful of my best friend. Besides, it's really bad form to insult the chef right before your party." Edna started to interrupt but I persisted. She could insult me—and did regularly—but she could not insult Jilly, my brilliant, kind and loyal friend. "Asher would be lucky to get her."

"True, I suppose," Edna said. "Asher would be lucky to get anyone. He's easy on the eyes but his brain stalled out in fifth grade. You Galloways all have stalling problems. That's why you can't drive that truck of yours."

"Again, I'd appreciate it if you'd keep these comments to yourself, at least until the event is over. I want to make this a five-star experience for your guests and I can't do that if I'm constantly dodging your arrows, Miss Evans."

"With that attitude it's no wonder Chief Harper let the soup cool between you," she said. "He needs a quiet girl, not someone who's always flapping like a fussy chicken and poking her beak where she doesn't belong."

Now Jilly pressed her finger to her lips. I forced a smile onto my face and into my voice. "It's so kind of you to think about Kellan's happiness, Miss Evans."

"I saw you two dancing around that campfire like randy teens," she said. "You and that mutt of yours are trying to bewitch him. But he deserves better than a Galloway, and I know you'll do the right thing and let him find the right girl. He's a decent man, Ivy, and in case the world hasn't shown you this, they are few and far between."

"Miss Evans?" Being polite took all the grit I had. "Why exactly are you calling? I'm set to pick you up in two hours."

"I just wanted to make sure you have everything I need. Pink grapefruit juice, pulp free. Grey Goose vodka, tangerine flavor. Macadamia nuts, unsalted. Salt makes my ankles swell."

"No one likes cankles," I said.

There was a long pause. "I suggest you shelve your so-called wit, Ivy. The Bridge Buddies will not find you at all amusing."

"Shame," I said. "Because I'll find them amusing."

"You'd be better off putting your energy into running into town for butterscotch hard candy. No toffee. It pulls out my dental plate. And there's a special conditioner waiting for me at the Crowning Glory salon."

I rolled my eyes. "This is like a rock star's rider."

Now the pause at the other end was pregnant with smug humor. I felt it, and Keats did, too, because his ruff lifted ever so slightly.

"Oh, Ivy. To you I *am* a rock star. I'm bringing your silly inn back from the brink of absolute doom with these guests. How else could you recover from the black cloud of murder hanging over that dump of a farm?"

Jilly used her free hand to gesture to her diaphragm. It was her signal for me to breathe deeply before speaking. That one little sign had saved me from stepping into some steaming piles of regret.

"It will be my great honor to serve you pulp-free grapefruit juice this weekend, Miss Evans."

"Make sure it's pink," she said. "The devil's in the details, Ivy."

"It sure is," I said.

"Now stop talking and make sure Sookie's nest is just as I told you. If one tiny thing changes, she won't lay. That hen is sensitive but also consistent when you attend to the details."

I reached into Sookie's nest box to collect the egg. "She's delivered, so I must be doing something right."

"That must be a comfort when you're doing so many things wrong. You're going to hear about many of them this weekend. The Bridge Buddies do not suffer fools kindly."

Jilly pretended to stab herself in the heart and I almost lost my composure.

"Gotta run, Miss Evans," I said. "I have an unexpected trip to town to fulfill your order."

"You should have asked me earlier," Edna said. "That's what professionals do. Right, Jillian? Or do they waste time making a mockery of their paying guests?"

Jilly gasped, giving herself away. "Right, Miss Evans. I've already ordered the crème brûlée, just as you asked.

"Monogrammed? I want this to be a very special experience for my guests... even if you ladies are making a joke out of it."

"No one's making a joke out of this event," I said. "In fact, it's deathly serious."

"I need to finish packing," Edna said. "But dare I suggest you avoid using the word 'deathly' this weekend? It sets the wrong tone."

I leaned over to set Sookie's perfect egg into the basket. "On that, at least, we're in full agreement."

CHAPTER TWO

Crowning Glory was my last stop before heading over to collect Edna. The salon wasn't open yet, but Robbi Ford, the owner, came to the door with Edna's hair conditioner. I was at a loss over how someone could look that perfect so early in the day. It was barely nine but her long, highlighted hair glistened in the sun and her makeup was on point. I supposed looking polished provided assurance to her clients that they were in good hands. She was probably in her mid-forties but looked younger than I felt at 33.

"Ivy, good luck this weekend," she said, handing me the conditioner. "I don't normally comment on my clients, but this group can be a little fractious. I'm sure your mother has mentioned that."

Nodding, I said, "Shields up."

"Do you have time for a quick trim?" she asked. "Great hair is half the battle with these ladies."

I backed away quickly. "I'm due to pick up Edna any moment. But thank you."

Poking her head out the door, she called after me, "It looks like it's been six months since your last confession... to a hair stylist."

"Eight," I called, grinning. "Farmers don't need to worry about their hair."

"Innkeepers might," she tried again. "A good cut just helps with your confidence."

"All good," I said, and then tripped over a pebble on the sidewalk. "But thanks."

Keats did a tight circle around me, seeming as anxious as I felt to get away. Spending time primping wasn't high on his to-do list either. There was nothing this dog hated more than a bath. Except maybe a cat.

Giving Robbi a last wave, I let Keats into my big black pick-up and went around to climb behind the wheel. With Robbi still at the door, I wanted nothing more than to sail off smoothly, but of course I stalled the truck as I pulled out. Lately I'd been doing better with the manual transmission but my nerves were showing.

"Maybe I'd drive better with a good haircut," I said, when I finally got the truck rolling. "Am I underestimating the value of vanity, Keats? Mom always says so."

He turned in the passenger seat and angled his head slightly to give me the full benefit of his honey-brown, sympathetic eye. He knew I was nervous. He knew my emotions almost before I had them. But he didn't enjoy being bounced around as I hip-hopped through Clover Grove. The jostling interrupted his close observation of local happenings.

It didn't do much for the upholstery under him, either. This truck had taken quite a beating since Hannah left it in my care. Luckily the animals she surrendered to me were in good shape.

"It's going to be fine, right?" I said. "It's just a bunch of bridge ladies. What could go wrong?"

Now he directed his blue eye at me, the one that seemed to penetrate to my soul. Then he mumbled something—a statement that ended with a whine.

I couldn't tell if it was a lament over all that had gone wrong before when it shouldn't have, or a warning not to get my hopes up. Bad luck had followed Keats and me since the day we met, like the dark clouds currently gathering overhead. I'd found the pup chained up and neglected in the yard of the man ultimately revealed to be a murderer. We nearly died in the fracas that followed. Then we moved here for the good life, and almost "bought the farm" again. Twice.

"Are you telling me not to be naïve?" I tried to focus on the stick shift. The ride through town, with stoplights and short turns, was the most challenging and frequently the most embarrassing. Everyone knew about my vehicular shortcomings.

Keats gave a quick, low swish and braced white paws on the dashboard, as if to help me pilot this big beast. It was strange how I managed to conceal my nerves from criminals, yet not while driving. The truck was a mood ring on wheels.

"I'll keep my eyes open, buddy," I said, as the truck lurched forward. "I realize the chances of our lives being all sunshine from here on in are slim. You and I rescued each other in dangerous circumstances. Maybe that wasn't a coincidence. It's hard not to look at what's happened since and wonder if fate had something bigger in mind for us." He didn't shift his gaze from the highway as we left town. True to his breed, he had a single-minded focus that was hard to shake. "Well, even if we're meant to deal with more crap together, I don't regret it for a single moment," I continued. "The life I lived before you wasn't much of a life at all, I realize now. It was all shades of grey." I dared a quick look around at the gorgeous fall leaves on trees both nearby and on the distant rolling hills. "That concussion I got when we took out your former owner brought out all the blazing color."

Keats pushed off the dashboard, turned and touched my wrist with his wet nose. It felt like a high five from the world's best dog, and my eyes filled instantly. My family and colleagues used to joke about my tear ducts being stitched shut. I had packed my emotions away behind a firewall so that I could downsize employees, earning the nicknames "killer" and "the grim reaper." After my conk on the head while rescuing Keats, however, the waterworks were never far away. I had to avoid letting myself feel too much gratitude, because it almost always led to involuntary public emissions. I'd cried in the hardware store, the butcher shop, and The Tipsy Grape. Especially The Tipsy Grape. I couldn't hold my liquor anymore, either. Teary moments weren't doing much for my already tattered reputation so now I tried hard to confine gratitude to our solitary walks in the meadows, where no one judged.

Rubbing my sleeve across my eyes, I bit my lip to bring myself back into the present as we turned into Edna's lane. There was no one more likely to exploit my weakness than Edna Evans. Despite that, I rather enjoyed sparring with her. It felt like visiting the gym to recover my strength. Going a few rounds with her regularly would ultimately build my capacity to deal with the other mudslingers in town.

I expected to see her waiting on the porch when we pulled up in front of her small tidy house, because I was two minutes late and she valued punctuality. Instead, she shouted for me to let myself in when I knocked. Her suitcase was sitting in the front hall but she was nowhere in sight.

"You're late," she called.

"So are you, apparently."

She walked into the living room and it struck me that she was moving more slowly and stiffly. Maybe her early trudge through the brush had caught up with her. But her hair was immaculately curled, if also a little stiff, and instead of the yellowed nursing uniform she usually wore around the house, she was in a floral dress with a similar print to the overstuffed chair she was standing beside.

"I've never liked leaving my home overnight," she said. "Especially since you moved into the neighborhood. That farm has been an eyesore and a hazard for years with all those rescue animals, but you've taken things to an extreme."

I pressed my lips together and forced them into a smile as stiff as Edna's new perm. It was just sparring, I reminded myself. There was a weary air about her today that suggested keeping the gloves up was tough work for her, too.

After a few seconds, my lips relaxed and I said, "I got your grapefruit juice and macadamia nuts. That should help."

"And the vodka?" she asked.

"Grey Goose tangerine, just like you asked." Tipping my head, I added, "A few weeks ago you said liquor had never touched your lips—and that's how you stayed so fresh and sharp."

She perched on the edge of the chair. "True for the most part. But when you meet the Bridge Buddies, you'll see that vodka is sometimes just medicine. The tangerine and grapefruit make it go down easier."

"They're really that bad?" I walked over to the couch and took a seat, without removing my boots. Edna had "accidentally" taken them hostage on a recent visit and now I didn't care what I tracked into her house. As if reading my mind, Keats gave a good scratch and sent some fur drifting into the sunbeams streaming across from the wall of windows where Edna liked to spy on us.

"They're not good," she said, frowning at Keats. "You had better be quick on your feet, Ivy Galloway. These are some of the smartest people in Clover Grove. It takes a sharp, analytical mind to play bridge at the level they do. In a different time and place, they'd have been business titans. Instead they were housewives who needed to channel their mental energy into strategy to avoid going insane in this town."

"You're the only one who had a career?" I asked.

Edna had worked for the only doctor in town for many decades, and had a side hustle as school nurse. She knew every nook and cranny in Clover Grove Elementary because she'd used her own strategic skills to hunt down every last student to vaccinate them with glee. My brother was usually the last because he spent the year sourcing new hiding places. One year he spent eight hours under the school stage, and all it got him was a heartier jab with Edna's savage syringe.

"I was the only one who didn't marry, so I had no choice in the matter." She stared at her sensible, rubber-soled black Mary Janes. "Although I came very close once."

"To marrying?" I tried to suppress my surprise but her gray eyebrows rose. I knew she'd found *my* hiding place and I'd be in for a sharp jab soon. "What happened?"

"I was jilted practically at the altar, I'm afraid." Leaning down, she tightened the strap on her shoe. "I don't really blame the man. There was a situation that reflected poorly on me. I wish he'd given me the benefit of the doubt, but it's long done."

"Is he still—" I was about to say alive but thought better of it. "In Clover Grove?"

"No," she said. "And yes, it's too late by more than fifty years. Don't get even softer just because you're working your wiles on Chief Harper."

"I have wiles?" I asked, smiling.

"You most certainly do. That's how you've managed to outwit a murderer or two. You and that mutt." She glared at Keats again. "I hope you've recharged because you'll need every trick up your sleeve to stay ahead of the Bridge Buddies."

I crossed my arms and leaned back. "You're likening your friends to murderers?"

She pushed herself upright and walked to the front hall. Opening the closet, she pulled out a wool coat, and then draped her rabbit pelt wrap over it. The rabbit hat came last, and she checked the mirror as she placed it gently on her curly hair. The smell of mothballs wafted toward me.

"Actually, yes," she said, at last. "Not literally of course, but they've murdered more reputations than you could ever imagine. You can't even get your hair set in this town without them convening the executive panel. Get the wrong verdict and you're on the bus to a salon in another town." Opening the front door, she turned. "Are you excited yet?"

A laugh slipped out and surprised me. I didn't think Edna had a real sense of humor. "Actually, no, Miss Evans. I'm filled with dread that deepens with every word. However, with Jilly and Keats backing me, I guess I'm a match for them. At least for three days."

She patted my back once as I passed in front of her and out the door. "Don't flatter yourself, young lady. And aren't you forgetting something?"

I turned on the porch to find her pointing to her suitcase. "At your service, madam."

We had a brief scuffle on the driveway when she refused to let me put the suitcase in the bed of the truck. "It'll get dusty," she said. "Your mutt can ride back there."

"My dog is not cargo and I won't risk his safety so that your suitcase stays pristine. Both can go in the back seat."

"I'll carry it in my lap," she said, trying to wrestle it away from me. All those years tussling with panicky children had kept her strong and fit.

"That's not safe, either," I said, giving up before one of us tripped.

"It would be perfectly safe if you knew how to drive this truck." Edna shoved me aside and somehow managed to clamber into the passenger seat with the suitcase and settle herself without my help. "All I ask is that you let me survive this short ride with my dentures intact. I dread to think what the ladies would say if I arrived toothless."

"Some of them are toothless themselves, guaranteed," I said, closing the door.

She rolled down the window to shout after me as I circled the truck. "That doesn't mean they can't bite."

"Like chickens," I said, climbing behind the wheel. "That's what you said earlier."

"Death by a thousand hen pecks," she said, with what may have been a sigh. Her suitcase was compressing her ribcage.

"You said not to joke about death this weekend," I reminded her.

"I'm not joking," she muttered. "Just telling my life story."

"It can't be that bad." I backed the truck around smoothly and headed slowly down the lane, easing over every pothole so that Edna wouldn't puncture a lung on the edge of her old-fashioned suitcase. "You're a survivor, Miss Evans. You've told me so yourself."

"Like a cockroach. Only tougher."

This time I guffawed. "Have you been into your tangerine medicine already? Don't do that while I'm driving."

Today I didn't stall, however. We rolled right on by the deep, marshy waterhole that Wilma, my sly sow, adored. Each time she escaped, she stopped by for a stinky wallow in what I now called the "pig pool." Once she took me with her and I almost stayed under... permanently.

The thought made me shudder, and that's why I didn't notice the truck shuddering before it made an ominous clunking sound and then tilted abruptly on the passenger side.

"I do believe you have a flat tire, Ivy. I hope you have a jack and a spare."

"I do. In the utility shed at the farm."

"Don't tell me you can't change a tire," she said. "It's a rite of passage for any teen in this county. You can't get your learner's permit without a parent vouching for that."

"That was nearly twenty years ago, Edna."

"Miss Evans," she corrected, her voice as crisp as the breeze coming through the window.

"Sorry." I smiled at her as I pulled out my phone. "I thought we just had a moment back there."

"We had a warning, not a breakthrough," she said. "Now, tell me how you intend to handle this so that we can get to the farm before my friends arrive."

I jumped out of the truck. "You said they're not friends."

"Friends, enemies... Who knows the difference anymore?"

Pressing a number in my contacts, I waited for the garage in town to answer. Fred, the owner, had sent his mechanic out for a recent tractor malfunction and convinced me to sign up for a service contract.

When I explained the problem today, he said, "What'd you hit?"

"Nothing that I know of." I circled the truck to the passenger side. "Uh-oh."

"What?" Edna demanded, although her voice was considerably weakened by the weight of the suitcase in her lap.

I knelt and looked around and under the truck. "Nails. Someone sprinkled a dozen or more big nails across your lane, Miss Evans."

If she responded, I didn't hear it because Fred was promising to arrive soon to remedy the problem.

Meanwhile, Edna had managed to push her suitcase into the driver's seat and open the passenger door.

"Stay inside," I said. "It's not safe in those shoes. You too, Keats."

She hopped out without hesitation. "Apparently it's not safe regardless. Someone must be targeting you on *my* property now. The audacity!"

"Why would they do that when they could just sprinkle nails in my own lane?" I asked, sighing.

"I can't explain your crazy life, Ivy. But you're the only one who drives in here."

I rolled my eyes at her. "Along with the cops. Kellan is here quite often. Maybe they're targeting him."

"Very funny." She picked her way around the truck carefully and pulled her suitcase out of the driver's seat, swinging it down without difficulty. "I'll walk to your place while you take care of this. I need to be there when the Bridge Buddies arrive."

"Edna, wait. You can't carry that on your own. Aren't you tired already after bushwhacking this morning?"

She turned, and her brow furrowed. "What are you talking about?"

"You know I saw you at my place earlier." I followed her and tried to take the suitcase. "Why did you take off into the bushes? You could have hurt yourself. It was barely light."

The handle slipped out of her fingers and her forehead creased into a tight, folded fan. "What are you on about, Ivy Galloway? People say you're brain-damaged, but this is the first I've seen of it."

All my years of interviewing in HR had taught me to look for the "tells." Even a skilled card player like Edna had them. Her lips puckered as if she'd jerked a drawstring and relaxed just as quickly. Then her throat clenched and her now-empty right hand clenched, too. She was definitely hiding something.

"I have a few loose screws after my accident, no question," I said, smiling. "But if you weren't visiting my henhouse before dawn this morning, I'll eat your rabbit hat."

Again her lips jerked into a tight pucker and her small eyes darted from side to side. "Well, if a woman can't visit her own hen now and then, perhaps those chickens should come home to roost. When this weekend is over, Sookie will join me. You can keep the others."

"Fine with me. I'd prefer you take her than risk sneaking

around in the dark and breaking a leg. Besides, you left the henhouse door ajar in your hurry to escape."

Now her whole face puckered and flushed till it looked like the apple head dolls they still sold at the fall fair. It took a few seconds before she croaked out, "Is Sookie okay?"

"Everything's fine and Charlie's already put a lock on the door."

Taking a step backward, she jerked the suitcase out of my hand so abruptly she broke one of my fingernails.

"Do not allow a fox in that henhouse before I can collect my Sookie." She turned to stride away, with that mere hint of a limp. "And once you attend to this flat, I'll thank you to mix my medicine before your guests arrive."

"Your friends, you mean," I called after her. "The reputation assassins."

Adjusting her rabbit hat with her free hand, she kept walking.

CHAPTER THREE

While Fred changed the tire in what seemed like an impossibly short time, I continued to search the lane for nails. I'd explained the task to Keats before Fred arrived, so that the mechanic wouldn't join the ranks of those questioning my sanity. The dog was a quick study, as always, and picked his way carefully up and down the lane. When he discovered a nail, he lifted one white paw in a point and stood perfectly still until I picked it up and dropped it into my clinking baseball cap.

By the time we were rolling again, I'd collected a couple of dozen.

"What do you make of that, Keats?" I asked. "Did I just get lucky driving in, or did someone scatter them while we were inside the house with Edna?"

Keats offered a mumbled commentary that ended with a squeak of a question mark. "I have no idea why someone would want to do that. With the way Edna was talking, she must have even more enemies than I already knew about. There's probably a club for people who despise Edna Evans for her nursing alone."

The dog braced himself on the dash and gave another mumble.

"No, I don't think it was about me, regardless of the timing.

Unless the Bridge Buddies wanted to keep me from arriving with Edna. Sounds like there's no love lost there."

Pulling up beside the barn, I saw four high-end SUVs. It looked like my guests had preceded me and they hadn't carpooled. It struck me as odd that none of them drove regular sedans, but maybe vehicles with more height were easier for senior citizens to climb into.

"All I'm saying is that this feels like a bad omen," I told Keats, as I turned off the truck. "But maybe I'm wrong. I've been wrong before."

This time Keats' commentary sounded indignant. "I didn't say *you've* been wrong before. Border collies are never wrong."

His mouth dropped open and his tongue lolled, and I shared the laugh. "We'll get through this, buddy. Let's just hope these ladies don't decide to murder my reputation just for sport. I doubt I'd offer enough challenge for the brightest women in town."

The guests had apparently just arrived because they were gathered on the wide front porch around Jilly. Edna was standing off to one side and her suitcase was sitting on the porch swing. She was wringing her hands, but I doubt anyone noticed but me. The others were chattering like birds that gathered before flying south for the winter. There were four gray heads with almost identical fluffy bouffants. I'd expected eight, but sprinkled among them were two dark male heads, a highlighted blonde and a petite brunette that barely reached shoulder level.

"Strange," I said, getting out of the truck. "Maybe they have chauffeurs."

Walking up the front stairs with Keats, I gave everyone my best innkeeper smile. "Welcome to Runaway Farm and Inn," I said. "I'm Ivy Galloway, and this is my wonder dog, Keats. You've obviously met Jilly Blackwood, my best friend and chef extraordinaire. Some of you know me, some of you don't, so I'd love it if we could do a quick round of introductions before you get you inside and settled."

The bridge club chair, Gertrude Boxton, stepped forward with her right hand outstretched. "I've known you since you were a wee mite," she said. "Although I could never tell you Galloway girls apart. Every last one of you looked the same. It was as if Dahlia had you cloned to avoid the wear and tear of pregnancy."

"I don't blame her if she did," Joan Snelling said. "I had three children before I moved to the spare room and put a lock on the door."

Everyone laughed, and I joined in although Joan herself wasn't smiling. She had very few lines on her face, although I knew they were all around 80. I guess her expressions didn't change often enough to leave a trail.

"I wish I'd thought of that," Annamae Muir added, taking her turn. "Five was one too many." She tipped her head and gave me a smile that looked more authentic than all the others combined. "The youngest is my favorite of course. I'm sure that's true in your family as well."

Before I could answer, the last woman stepped forward. Morag Tanner was tall and almost masculine in her austerity. The others still had a bit of pepper in their salty hair, but Morag's was snow white and I knew it took work to keep it that way.

"Oh come now, Annamae," she said, rolling her eyes. "Everyone knows Asher Galloway is Dahlia's favorite. In fact, everyone in hill country has a weakness for that handsome young man. I've been trying to pair my granddaughter up with him. He needs to settle down with a nice, local girl."

The others murmured agreement.

I glanced at Jilly. Her face had flushed to the roots of her cascading blonde curly hair and her eyes dropped to her striped apron. Behind her, Edna Evans gave a chuckle with a hint of malice. Her eyes met mine with a silent "I told you so."

"As far as I know I'm not cloned," I said. "Mom says my delivery was like passing a set of broken china."

The four women winced, no doubt remembering their own childbirth ordeals. Edna, on the other hand, smirked.

"Well, you've certainly made that push worthwhile, Ivy," Gertrude said. Her blue eyes were all the brighter for her pale skin. These women spent most of their time inside playing cards and it showed. Maybe that's why they all looked significantly younger than Edna. Either that or her nasty feats had caught up with her.

Money never hurt either when it came to keeping age at bay. These women could afford the best products, spa visits and maybe even a tuck here and there, if they could tear themselves away from their games. If so, vanity didn't show in their wardrobe selections. All wore black pants, a white shirt and a maroon jacket with the bridge club emblem stitched into the breast pocket.

"You've done well for yourself," Joan said.

"Very well," Annamae echoed.

"Some people have all the luck," Morag added.

I wondered if they always spoke in this precise order. Maybe that was in the club's founding rules.

"I have been lucky," I replied. "Wrong place wrong time, initially. Now that's reversed."

"Rescuing that dog was terribly risky," Gertrude said.

"Dangerous," Joan said.

"Terrifying," Annamae added.

"Reckless," Morag said, with the finality of a gavel coming down. "Dahlia must have used up the common sense on the rest of the family."

If they were trying to get under my skin, they'd have to work harder than that. "Oh come now, Morag. You know full well there are more reckless Galloways than me." It was true, too. My sister Poppy in particular was a wild child who'd kept the town talking for decades.

"You used to be so quiet," Gertrude said. "I wondered if you were right in the head. Then you got that fancy-pants job in the city and I realized you got all the brainpower the others lacked. But then you spun things around again with one reckless move. You could have lost everything, Ivy."

"Instead I gained it." I gestured to the beautifully renovated century-old farmhouse. The extension at the back of the house had a more modern design with plenty of large windows.

"I don't know what Hannah Pemberton was thinking," Gertrude said.

"Or drinking," Joan began, but I cut the cycle short.

"She was thinking I would adore her animals and protect them with my life if I had to," I said. "Unfortunately, I've had to."

"You didn't have to, you chose to." The voice came from the porch swing, where Edna had now perched beside her suitcase. "You could have just left everything to the police. In fact, I heard Chief Harper ask you himself to leave things alone. Instead you put yourself in harm's way again and again."

My eyes met Jilly's and although her own color was still high, she gestured toward her diaphragm. Deep breaths, I told myself. The Bridge Buddies had come prepared to try me in the court of Clover Grove public opinion and there was likely no winning.

Well, if I couldn't beat them at their own game, I knew I'd better get them to the tables we'd set up in the family room as soon as possible. Once they focussed on their true passion in life, they'd likely abandon their assault on mine.

"Jilly's made a lovely buffet lunch you can eat in the family room as you prepare," I said. "I know why you're really here and that's not to make small talk about my peccadilloes."

"Peccadilloes," Annamae echoed. "That's such a funny word, isn't it?"

She covered her mouth, realizing even before Morag turned that she'd spoken out of order.

"I just have one question," I continued. "I see some unfamiliar faces. Gertrude, could you please introduce the other guests?"

Through this entire conversation, four people had remained utterly silent, as if commanded never to speak.

Gertrude hesitated for a moment before gesturing to the lanky man beside her. He appeared to be about 30, with a wispy beard that probably couldn't be coaxed to do more. "This is Ricardo Lima."

Joan introduced Solomon Dean, an older gentleman with an aggressive gray beard, a smooth bald head, and eyes that twinkled like Charlie's, my silver fox farm manager. Annamae sounded girlishly bashful as she introduced the fortyish blonde, Stacy Willis. And Morag wasn't bashful at all as she nodded to her companion, Kimberly Stetts, a woman who was probably around 60, with a similar serious, masculine air about her.

I thanked them and let Jilly and Keats herd them inside. Edna hung back, no doubt waiting for me to take care of her suitcase.

"What's with these mystery guests?" I asked, once everyone was out of earshot. "I expected eight Bridge Buddies. Have you lost some club members recently?"

Edna gave me a "duh" look that didn't quite suit an octogenarian's face. "Ivy, do you know nothing at all about bridge? I would have thought you'd at least do some research before your guests arrived."

A pinprick of shame bloomed in my chest. Normally I *would* do that type of research, but it was struggle enough to get the latest episode of murder cleared up and cover the basics of innkeeping and farm management.

"You're right, Edna," I said, sensing it was something she couldn't hear often enough. "I should have done my homework. Especially when games of chance have never been my strong suit."

"Again, that statement shows how little you know. Bridge is far from a game of chance. As I said earlier, it's all about strategy, and some of the most brilliant minds in the world compete just to get into elite bridge clubs. In big cities, you need references, proof that you've studied under a master, and an impressive audition. The best players have tutors so they never stop learning."

"Ah, so the four strangers are bridge tutors?"

Edna gave a cluck that was the equivalent of "duh." Checking to make sure everyone was safely inside, she whispered, "Don't be so naïve. Those people are their partners."

"Partners!" I stared at her while imagining 80-year-old Gertrude in a compromising position with young Ricardo. "Oh. Well, that seems a bit strange."

"It's not strange at all in the bridge world. Although I concede it's probably rare in Clover Grove. That's why I suggested holding the tournament out here at your farm. There's no one around to ask impertinent questions. We can't afford gossip."

"No, I can certainly see that. The Bridge Buddies are all married."

"As are their partners, I believe." Edna crossed her arms. For the first time I noticed she'd removed her rabbit accoutrements in favor of the maroon bridge club jacket, which clashed with her floral print dress. "I don't see what that has to do with anything."

My own brow felt as furrowed as hers had been earlier. I blamed Flordale Corporation for stealing my youth. Sometimes I looked at my fresh-faced sisters and wondered if I looked like the oldest. The clone that was wearing out before its time.

"Well, I'm not one to judge," I said at last. "Extramarital affairs are nothing new to me. There were plenty of shenanigans like that in my old company. I just didn't expect my inn to turn into a bridge club love shack."

"Love shack!" Edna's voice rose.

I pressed my finger to my lips and then continued. "It's all fine between consenting adults. But now I understand why you wanted to sit this game out."

"Consenting adults? What are you on about, Ivy Galloway?"

"There's quite an age gap between Gertrude and Ricardo. Stacy is half Annamae's age as well, but whatever. I'm certainly no ageist, Miss Evans, but I can't help wondering if money is changing hands."

"Of course it is," she hissed. "Partners like these don't come cheap and they charge a pretty penny. They're elite pros, make no mistake."

I was starting to feel uncomfortable. Though far from a prude, the idea of paid arrangements like this under my roof when husbands were a short drive away made me shake my head.

"Stop shaking your head like that," Edna said. "You'll injure your brain even more. If you want to work in hospitality, you need to adjust to surprises like this. You get paid for your discretion."

I switched from shaking to nodding. "I guess I will need to adjust my expectations. I wanted to market the sweet farm experience, not the illicit tryst experience." Setting the suitcase down, I stared at Edna. "Just to make perfectly sure I understand you... Ricardo is a gigolo hired by Gertrude for a recreational weekend?"

Edna's purse string mouth had gone slack, and then her lips smacked together before words came out. "Ivy Rose Galloway. If you're suggesting what I think you are, I will wash your mouth out with soap. In fact, I will dip your brain into disinfectant with my own bare hands."

Her gnarled fingers twitched as if itching to get on with it.

"You're the one who said they're having secret extramarital affairs with paid partners," I said. "That sounds like gigolo territory to me."

Her eyes closed and her lips puckered again. Then she covered her mouth and her shoulders started shaking under her maroon club jacket. "Oh my goodness," she said, at last. "I don't know whether to thank you or kick you for the images running through my mind right now. Morag and Kimberly. Oh my, oh my."

I had never heard Edna Evans laugh before. There had been plenty of snickers and guffaws at my expense, but never a true belly laugh. She braced herself against the house and let it rip. It was a good minute before she stopped long enough for me to ask, "What's so funny?"

"Ivy, you stupid girl, these are *bridge partners*. Professionals who pair with a club member and increase the level of play. Sometimes they sit in while the club members rest. I can't afford a ringer's fees, which is why I'm not participating in this tournament. We've only been able to hold these events out of county in the past, to avoid looking pretentious and extravagant. Your farm gives us the privacy to play higher stakes bridge near home."

"Well, how was I supposed to know?" I said, heaving a sigh of relief. As much as I didn't want to judge, I also didn't want to be the keeper of sordid secrets for the town. I was fine with keeping my lips sealed about paid bridge ringers.

"You spent a decade in Boston," Edna said. "I thought you'd be more worldly."

"Well, you were a public health nurse," I said. "I thought you'd be more worldly about cross-generational affairs."

Color flooded her face and seemed to build pressure until she started laughing helplessly again. "I do wish I could share this story," she said.

"What story?" someone asked behind us. "Edna, are you all right? You look like you're going into cardiac arrest."

Gertrude's sharp eyes ran over us top to bottom, searching for clues.

"It's my fault, I'm sorry," I said. "I was just telling her about an accident I had with manure recently. Would you like to hear it?"

"No, I would not," Gertrude said. "But I would like to know why the police are coming down your lane. We value our privacy."

That set Edna off again and she collapsed onto the swing fanning herself before the police SUV was even parked.

CHAPTER FOUR

There was a time in my past when the sight of a police car generated moderate anxiety. Depending on what I was doing at the time, I may have wondered if I'd been speeding or had inadvertently cut someone off. Or I'd wonder if there'd been an accident or a crime. Boston had no shortage of reasons for police cars to cruise into view.

Now, just two months into my move to Clover Grove, the arrival of a squad car flooded me with a strange mix of emotions. Warm fondness, because my brother, an officer, spent a lot of time on the farm. Worry, in case something else had gone wrong around the farm. And now, most predominantly, a fizz of excitement. As much as I loved my brother, I wanted it to be Kellan Harper behind the wheel. Taking that one step further, I wanted Chief Harper to be visiting as regular civilian Kellan, my former high school sweetheart and new-again friend.

"Ivy," Gertrude said. "Snap out of that trance. I know you've got your eye on Kellan—every red-blooded woman in town does. At least if they favor tall, dark and handsome over your beach boy brother. But we booked your inn for the privacy, and we don't want cops hanging around."

"I'm sure it's a social visit," I said. "We don't have police business at the moment."

"You always seem to have police business," Gertrude said. "I don't know why I let you talk me into this, Edna. Discretion is of the utmost importance during a tournament."

The police car stopped near the barn and Kellan got out. He raised his arm in a wave and flashed white teeth in a way that suggested the visit wasn't anything too serious. I waved back, trying to keep it casual. My heart had started jumping like the three baby pygmy goats in their pen. They were always hopping around their playset as if jacked up on drugs. I'd seen creatures do some strange things since moving here, but nothing was crazier than baby goats. Just thinking of them made me smile.

Keats smiled too, because he loved practicing his herding moves on Kellan, much to the chief's dismay. Kellan wasn't a fan of animals, which was definitely a sticking point between us. I was sure he could be converted eventually.

"Wipe that smile off your face," Edna said. "Never give away your entire hand like that. Now Kellan has the advantage."

"I was thinking about baby goats," I said. "Have you been down to see them? I dare you not to smile."

"That's a dare you'd lose," Edna said. "Anyway, control your merriment and keep the man guessing."

"Get rid of him," Gertrude said. "If we wanted exposure, we could have just used the bridge club building in town instead of paying for—"

"Privacy," I said, pronouncing the word her way, as if it had an extra v. "I don't understand the secrecy, Mrs. Boxton. It's a high stakes game with skilled players. Unless it requires a human or animal sacrifice, there's nothing to hide."

Gertrude sniffed. "You understand nothing about our world, Ivy. We're pillars of the community, so we can't afford gossip."

"What's to gossip about?" I asked, wondering why Kellan was staying near the barn instead of coming up to the porch.

"You do realize my son-in-law is the mayor of this town," Gertrude said. "There's more pressure on me to behave with propriety than most people. Some might say our tournaments are extravagant and wasteful."

"It's your money. You should be able to spend it as you like."

"Indeed," Gertrude said. "But you more than anyone should understand what the grapevine is like around here."

I sighed. "Yeah. How about I go down to see what Kellan wants and hurry him along?"

"You do that," Gertrude said.

"No fawning," Edna added. "Treat men like dogs, Ivy. Just a little reward here and there to reinforce good behavior. In fact, you want to randomize it, so they never know if they're going to get a smile and keep working. Consistency is necessary with children but the reverse is true with grown men."

I started down the stairs, shaking my head. The day I took romantic advice from Edna Evans was the day I surrendered the farm. In other words, never. "Why don't you ladies head inside and get settled?" I called back.

Gertrude actually did as I asked, but Edna sat down on the swing yet again.

"And leave you alone with the police chief?" she said. "I don't think so. You need a chaperone."

She pushed off with one Mary Jane, and the very first swoosh brought her suitcase crashing down.

I stopped at the bottom of the stairs. "A chaperone? I'm thirty-three years old."

"With a brain permanently stalled in puberty," Edna said. "I was your school nurse, remember? I saw how you hung off Kellan's every word, as if he were chief already. He knows he can get away with sprinkling a few crumbs for you, when you should be demanding the entire cake."

Turning, I went back up the stairs. "Miss Evans. Please keep your voice down. I appreciate commentary on my innkeeping skills. Beyond that, I'm good."

"Oooh, snippy," Edna said, pushing off again. "Just trying to offer perspective from someone who learned from heartbreak. But if you can afford to lose Kellan again, by all means ignore me."

"Deep breaths," I said aloud as I started back down the stairs. "Keats, give me strength."

"I wouldn't chat so much to your dog, either," she called after me. "Men like Kellan don't like crazy women."

"My mom said otherwise." I regretted the words the moment they were out. Before my concussion I would never have blurted something like that to someone like Edna. Or anyone else for that matter. The specialists had said it would take a minimum of a year and a maximum of never before the "insult" to my brain healed. So I'd just have to do my best with my flawed impulse control.

"Did she now?" Edna called over the squeak of the porch swing. I'd have to get Charlie to come up with some oil. That squeaking and squawking would get old fast. "Well, Dahlia is quite a success story with men, isn't she?"

I winced as my feet hit the flagstone walk. Defending my mother didn't come easily. She'd been single a long time after my deadbeat father left her to raise six kids on her own. A series of low-end jobs that she kept losing didn't give her much leisure for romance, even with my eldest sister Daisy shouldering most of the parenting load. Now that Mom was free as a bird, however, she'd taken up what she called "rotational dating," and had become the talk of the town. Even more so than usual. All the term meant was that she had a "stable" of eligible men with varied interests and could be busy every night of the week if she chose. One man in her stable was none other than my silver fox farm manager, Charlie, which made me more uncomfortable than the idea of the bridge club gigolos earlier. It was just too close for comfort.

"Miss Evans, let's leave my mother out of this, shall we?"

"You brought her into it, Ivy. I'm just pointing out that following her example might not bring the results you want with Kellan."

I crossed my arms and turned to seize the bait. "And following your advice will? You were complaining about being single this very morning."

"I'm single by choice, young lady. I had my opportunities—I was a very pretty girl—but sadly, I lost the one I truly wanted. My soul mate, as it were. Everything after that was just slumming as far as I was concerned so I didn't bother. Tell me that wouldn't be the case for you with Kellan, and I will happily stand down and let you take your chances with Dahlia's advice." The squeaking stopped suddenly. "Why, speak of the devil."

"No!" I turned so fast my hair swung into my face and obscured my vision. When the dark cloud settled, I saw my Mom's ancient yellow Volvo coming up the lane at a sedate pace. "What is she doing driving?"

"I thought they took her license away," Edna said. "I heard Asher was a laughing stock because of her antics behind the wheel."

Indeed, Mom's scattered focus had resulted in the premature death of a few stop signs. With fines piling up and the threat of an actual body count to follow, Kellan had assigned Asher to seize her plates. As far as I knew, the car itself was stashed with one of Asher's buddies. It had been like a pet to Mom so he couldn't bear to sell it.

When the yellow car swung up in front of the house in an elegant arc, I knew Mom couldn't be behind the wheel. In fact, her face was pressed to the passenger window and the door opened quickly. Asher leapt from the driver's side and circled at a run, but

Mom was like a cat—swift, agile and graceful. She'd taken up yoga a year ago at the behest of an attractive young instructor who may well have been in her rotation.

"Mom, what are you doing here?" I said, heading back up the stairs once more to act as a human shield to my guests.

She swept up the stairs as if they were her own personal catwalk. Indeed, she was dressed to impress in a formfitting knit dress in red—her signature color—accessorized with a black cashmere cardigan, and black patent heels. "Is that any way to greet your mother, Ivy? You were always the sweetest of my girls. I don't know what happened."

"Getting bashed on the head is what happened," Edna offered, as the swing started squeaking again.

"You may be right, Edna," Mom said. "How are you? You look a little tired."

"And you don't look tired at all," Edna said. "Which is surprising."

It was the delicate art of jab and parry that Clover Grove girls learned early, at the skirts of their mothers. At least most did. I seemed to have taken most of my life lessons from my next sibling in line, namely Asher.

He came after Mom now, mouthing "sorry" to me.

"My guests just arrived, Mom," I said. "So I don't have time to chat."

She smiled up at me. At barely five feet tall, she had nonetheless produced good-sized humans. I was the tallest of the girls and Asher was well over six feet. "Darling, maybe you'll find time for your mother when you discover she's come bearing gifts."

Her hands were empty. "What gifts?"

Kellan was now nearly at the stairs, aided in his journey—or impeded, depending how you looked at it—by a black-and-white whirlwind. Keats had apparently left tiny punctures in every pair of Kellan's uniform pants. Meanwhile, Asher's uniforms went unmolested.

"Leave it, Keats," I said, and the dog fell back, his tail drooping in disappointment.

"Mom is giving you Buttercup," Asher said, grinning.

"*Lending* you Buttercup," Mom corrected. "Chief Harper is concerned about your driving, Ivy. I'm afraid the apple doesn't fall far from the tree. So Asher suggested we bring Buttercup out of retirement for the good of the community."

Heat rose from the pit of my stomach, and I circulated my glare from Mom to Asher and finally to Kellan. "I do not need an old yellow jalopy, thank you very much. My stick handling is quite good now."

"You stalled twice this morning," Edna said, over swing squeaks. "I was afraid for my life."

"You should be afraid for your life if someone is spiking your driveway with nails," I said.

"Spiking her driveway?" Kellan said, his brilliant smile fading. "What happened, Miss Evans? And why hasn't this been reported?"

"It was just an hour or so ago," I said, gesturing to an old tin can sitting near the corner of the porch. "There's the evidence."

Edna pushed herself off the swing and there was a little wobble in her walk. I wondered if Jilly had already served her some vodka medicine. "I'm quite sure those nails were intended for Ivy," she told Kellan. "She's the one using my driveway all the time." She buttoned her bridge club blazer. "Maybe they wanted to take your truck out of commission, Ivy. I can only hope they'll be kinder to Buttercup."

Mom turned on Asher. "You told me my car would be in safe hands. I was worried about something like this happening. Ivy is a trouble magnet."

"I manage to keep dozens of animals alive, Mom, so I'm sure I can keep Buttercup safe, too." I looked down at the old sedan and sighed. I liked to fly under the radar and that was difficult enough before Buttercup. There wasn't a more conspicuous car in town.

The screen door opened and the four Bridge Buddies, followed by Jilly, joined Edna and Mom on the porch. I noticed the ringers had been kept inside. Perhaps they were stashed in closets to avoid gossip.

"Why, Dahlia, we were just talking about you," Gertrude said. There was a slight edge to her tone to let Mom know nothing pleasant had been said. "We were commenting that it seemed impossible you produced six children. And now look at you. No one else your age could get away with a dress like that."

"Wherever did you find it?" Joan asked. No doubt they knew full well that Mom's fashion finds came from secondhand stores around hill country. She avoided buying locally in case she happened to show up at an event like this wearing someone's castoff, skillfully altered.

"I never could wear something like that," Annamae said, sounding genuinely admiring. "You look lovely, Dahlia."

"Scarlet certainly is your color," Morag finished, with a sly smile.

"Thank you so much, ladies." Mom's fixed smile confirmed she felt the barbs but that her defences were holding. "You look lovely, too. Those uniforms are so sensible. You never even need to think about what to wear. It must be so freeing."

I winced and Kellan noticed. His head swivelled back and forth with each volley from the ladies, whereas Asher seemed oblivious to the politics. With Jilly nearby, my brother had a hard time focusing at the best of times. He gazed at her raptly now and she finally tore her horrified gaze away from the sparring women to give him a quick smile. He stood a little taller and his shoulders went back. Maybe Edna was right about a little going a long way with men. It wasn't a strategy with Jilly, however. She had a natural ease with men and hadn't been single for such a long stretch since we'd met in college. Having committed to helping me get the inn off the ground, however, she wasn't going to be diverted by a handsome man. She had all the focus my brother lacked, and that would stand him in good stead if he played his cards right.

"Who's doing your hair now?" Gertrude asked. "I know you had to part ways with Robbi at Crowning Glory. I'm sure it's been difficult."

"It's an interesting new look," Joan said.

"Lovely and unique," Annamae added.

"I've never seen a color quite like it," Morag finished.

"Ladies, you do flatter me," Mom said. "And while I love that, I heard you shut me out of Crowning Glory. Apparently I took one of your standing appointments once too often and suddenly, I was on my own holding a box of hair color."

"I don't know what you're talking about," Gertrude said. "Although I am unhappy when I can't get my weekly set. I've been seeing Robbi for more than a decade, and she does treat her regulars like gold." She turned quickly. "That reminds me, Edna. You pushed Annamae out of her regular spot with an impromptu permanent yesterday."

Edna flushed a maroon almost as deep as her club blazer and touched her tight curls. "It was a last-minute decision. I didn't realize it bumped you, Annamae."

"It was fine," Annamae said. "It doesn't hurt me to do my own hair now and then."

"Yes it does," Gertrude said. "You have arthritis, Annamae. When it flares up from overuse, your game suffers. I'm sorry to say that, but Edna needs to know the implications of her sudden whims."

Now Annamae flushed as bright as Edna, no doubt feeling she'd let down the team.

Morag shook her head. "No one gets perms anymore, Edna. What were you thinking?"

"I just wanted it to be low maintenance this weekend," Edna said. "A perm is set-and-forget."

"You're not even playing," Gertrude said. "But now Annamae's performance could decline."

Edna rose from the swing and walked over to the group. "Well, what are partners for?"

There was a collective gasp among the fearsome four, which made Kellan, Jilly and me jump. Asher continued to smile happily, as if social annihilation weren't underway. Mom, on the other hand, had a small, sly smile, delighted the heat was off her.

In the momentary silence, Keats circled Kellan, trying to rope him into doing something. Kellan's handsome face had a horrified expression I'd never seen before. Clearly he was new to the politics of the Clover Grove female old guard. They were the meanest of mean girls, with the power associated with their husbands' wealth.

We exchanged a helpless glance and I shrugged slightly to let him know there was nothing the chief of police could do to stop the massacre. Annamae dabbed at her eyes with an embroidered handkerchief but Edna was stoic. Only the fact that her lips were pressed in a firm seal, rather than a pucker of disapproval, gave her distress away.

"Mrs. Galloway, we really must be going," Kellan said. "We'll leave Buttercup in Ivy's capable hands and drop you back at your place."

At Keats' urging, Kellan walked up the stairs and offered my mother his arm. She took it, saying, "You can leave me at The Tipsy Grape, if you don't mind, Chief Harper. I'm meeting a friend."

You had to know my mother well to realize the throwaway comment was an act of true kindness to me. Gertrude, Joan and Morag all turned away from Annamae and Edna to exchange disgusted looks over my mother's wanton ways. It gave them a new focus instead of Edna's perm, which really didn't look bad at all. Perms had come a long way.

"Thank you, Mom," I called after her. "That was really good of you."

She turned and gave me an arch smile. "I do what I can for my favorite daughter. Now take good care of my sweet Buttercup. Treat her as well as this shaggy mutt of yours."

Keats trotted beside her, tail lashing in a most undignified way. Regardless of Mom's quirks, he adored her. I could only assume he sensed she'd delivered me into the world, because he didn't show that sloppy affection to anyone else... even me.

Opening the rear passenger door, Kellan helped Mom into the police car. "Officer Galloway, let's go," he called. "On the job, remember."

"Get along now, Asher," Gertrude said. "I don't feel safe knowing how far gone you are over Ivy's kitchen help. You look like a lovestruck goat. There are so many local girls who'd suit you better."

"You're wrong, Mrs. Boxton," he said, completely unfazed. "And I bet Mr. Boxton still looks at you exactly the same way."

Gertrude's mouth snapped shut and stayed that way until the SUV disappeared down the lane in a cloud of dust.

CHAPTER FIVE

E dna refused repeated offers of her medicinal vodka, barely touched her dinner and didn't lift a spoon to slice through the ornate letter E on the crème brûlée made with eggs from her very own hens. The scorching shame heaped on her over a simple perm seemed to have diminished her in ways that being accused of colluding with a murderer hadn't. Being nearly a pariah among her peers had clearly taken more of a toll than her rabbit pelts suggested.

I wasn't terribly surprised when she told me she wanted to go home. The conversation over dinner had been light, fast and full of mostly harmless gossip. My head ached from the speed of the over-lapping—if orderly—voices. Initially I assumed they just wanted to get to their evening game, but then I noticed that while Annamae was permitted to speak, whenever Edna tried to pipe in, she was summarily shut down. As the host, I tried to draw Edna out and was summarily shut down as well. Keats sat like a black-and-white statue by my side, directing his blue eye warily around the room. His ruff rose and settled with the waves of hostility. They were just as palpable to me.

"You're sure?" I asked, hauling Edna's suitcase down the stairs and over to Buttercup.

"Yes, I'm sure. I told you I didn't like being away from home."

"You also told me you wanted to be here supervising my every move."

"Supervising you is tiring," she said, letting me open the door for her. "You make so many gaffes. And getting waited on loses its appeal rather quickly."

I rolled my eyes as I put the suitcase in the back seat and then walked around the old sedan. I let Keats in on the other side, and then slid behind the wheel. Everything was adjusted for my tall brother, so I had to find the lever and then fiddle with the mirrors as well. "Okay, old girl," I said. "Ready for take off."

"Don't you dare call me that." Edna's voice was all sharp edges.

I glanced over at her. "Lighten up. I was speaking to Buttercup."

She fussed for a moment with her rabbit wrap. "The way you carried on, it was like preparing for an expedition to Mars."

"We just completed a strange mission," I said, piloting the big yellow car down the dim driveway. It got dark so early now. Even with our early dinner, night would fall over the farm like a black drop cloth very soon. "What was with those ladies? I told Jilly to spike their breakfast with some cannabis."

"You didn't!" Edna was scandalized. "That would completely throw off their game."

"But they'd be happier. And nicer."

"Bridge isn't about being happy and nice," Edna said. "It's about cutthroat cunning."

"Apparently. I don't often feel sorry for my mother, but today they left her in tatters."

"She's wise to wear red if she's going to bait the Bridge Buddies," Edna said. "Hides the blood."

I laughed, glad she seemed to be perking up a bit. "They were hard on you, too. Seems like they made an awfully big deal about a hair appointment."

She turned on me with the swiftness of a viper. "What do you know? My mistake probably caused Annamae to lose her competitive edge. She paid a lot for that partner, and now she won't get the lift she deserves."

"I think you're being a little hard on yourself," I said, turning onto the highway.

"And I think you should be a little harder on yourself. How can you improve if you let yourself off the hook all the time? Or worse, let Kellan Harper get you off the hook."

I drew a deep breath in through my nose. "I hope no one's dropped by with another bag of nails. It's tough getting new tires for vintage cars."

"This thing is ridiculous," Edna said. "It's going to break down all over town, just like it did on your mother. She was always playing the helpless female and getting men to repair it. It's important to be self-sufficient in life. I never took a dollar I didn't earn."

I let the arrow fly. My mom currently allowed the six of us to subsidize her rent and other needs. No matter how hard she tried— and she probably hadn't tried that hard—she couldn't hold down a job for long. There was no regular income, other than what we pitched in. I had covered her rent for years, and my siblings did what they could. At least mom knew how to squeeze a penny till it squeaked.

"It *is* good to be self-sufficient," I said, to mollify her. "You should be proud of what you've accomplished."

"I am. Did you know that I can shoot a crossbow? And light a fire without matches?"

"Really? That's impressive. You're all set for the zombie apocalypse."

"Laugh all you like, but if that happens, they'll come for people like you first." She leaned forward and stared at the road, likely looking for nails. "You can't even drive your own vehicle. Instead you took mommy's handout."

Another deep breath. Two. Three. The Bridge Biddies had slung a lot of manure and now it was rolling downhill.

"Did your folks teach you how to fend for yourself in the wilderness?" I asked.

She sniffed a negative. "I taught myself everything I know. Nothing was given to me. Ever. Unlike you, swanning in here on a magic carpet unfurled by Hannah Pemberton."

"I *have* been lucky," I said. "At least lately. But I intend to work hard and contribute fully to this community, Miss Evans. And before you know it, I'll be delivering your crème brûlée in my truck again. This is just to tide me over till I can get a few private lessons. I'm good at a lot of things, but driving stick isn't one of them."

I used to think my strongest superpower was managing people, but today I'd been thoroughly rousted by the Bridge Buddies and Edna. Maybe I'd be better off leaving the inn in Jilly's charge and sticking to managing the livestock. Most of them cooperated with me. Or at least the long arm of my law, in the form of Keats.

Pulling up in front of Edna's darkened house, I turned off the car and reached for my door handle.

"Don't bother," she said. "I can handle my own luggage. Ride your golden goose back to the farm and leave me in peace."

There was a little whine behind me as Keats tried to seal my lips, but a few hot ones came steaming out. "Wow, you're outdoing yourself tonight, Miss Evans. I know getting treated like crap by your friends stung, but stinging everyone else won't make you feel better."

She got out quite easily and bent to look back in. "That's where you're wrong. I feel better already."

"All right then. You enjoy that crème brûlée. Hope it sweetens you up a little before I come back in the morning."

Setting the treat on the porch stair, she came back to collect her suitcase. "Back off," she barked at Keats. "You're not a person, you know. No matter what goes on between you two wack jobs."

I turned in time to see Keats flinch away from her energy. We both wanted to curl up like hedgehogs.

"Night," I said. "I'll be here by eight to grab you in time for breakfast."

"Make it seven thirty," she said, struggling to pull out her suitcase. Once it was on the ground, she slammed the back door and prepared to do the same with the front. "I've got news for you, Ivy Galloway." She pinned me with her intense, small eyes that looked like black holes. "No matter how long you're here or how much you contribute, you will never belong. So get used to standing on your own."

"Will do," I said, offering a salute. "Can I borrow your crossbow?"

She slammed the door so hard Buttercup rattled and Keats unleashed an unearthly howl.

"It's okay, buddy," I said as he slid between the seats and sat beside me. I turned the key and then ran my hand over his sleek fur again and again. "Hurt people hurt people. So we need to cut them some slack." Putting the car in gear, I headed back down the lane. "But after this weekend, Edna can cook her own darn meals until she grows some manners."

———

THE NEXT MORNING, Buttercup refused to turn over. I got out of the bright yellow car and paced for a moment with Keats, before deciding to make the journey to Edna's in the golf cart Hannah had used before she mastered standard transmission. It had its own shed beside the barn, not far from the henhouse.

"If it was good enough for Hannah, it's good enough for me," I told Keats as we headed around to get the cart.

That way I'd head off Edna's snarky comments about being stalled in perpetual adolescence. On top of that, I could see any nails in the road more easily and avoid getting Fred out from town so early.

"It's going to be a good day," I told Keats as he hopped in beside me, tongue lolling. He loved the golf cart because he could catch every last whiff of whatever smelled good to a sheepdog, which was pretty much anything. His head tipped back as we whipped down the lane and he dug in his claws as I swerved to miss the potholes. "I'm going to hit every one on the way back, though. Consider yourself warned."

Edna deserved a very bumpy ride after her comments the night before. To make sure of it, I took the side trails through the bushes to seek out the worst possible ride. My own head was pounding when I pulled out of the bush practically at Edna's doorstep.

I'd expected to find her on the porch tapping her watch, but she was still inside. Keats and I ran up the stairs. I knocked twice and then opened the door and called, "Your chariot awaits, Miss Evans. I hope you had a great night's sleep and are ready for round two with your Bridge Buddies."

There was no answer so we stepped into the front hall. "Miss Evans? Yoo-hoo!" And then just, "Edna?"

Silence. For a chilling moment I wondered if she'd done something drastic, but then shook off the worry. Like Edna had said herself, she was like a cockroach. Tough and resilient. This morning she'd be fresh and ready to kick some biddy butt.

I walked through the small house, poking my head into each of the two bedrooms. Both exploded with floral fabric, similar to the living room upholstery. The master had a canopy and a row of dolls lounging against the pillows. Their eyes seemed to follow me when I walked through to check the en suite.

Keats looked up at them and whined.

"I know. Creepy, right?"

After that, we went to the kitchen. My footsteps were quicker now as I started to worry again. Had Edna fallen? Was she in the basement under a bookcase? Or in the yard stuck in a gopher hole with a broken leg?

I should have brought the truck after all. How was I going to get her out of here in a golf cart?

Keats turned up his blue eye and mumbled.

"Right," I said. "I'd call 911, of course. Transportation is their problem. Discovery is mine."

My heart was racing by the time we walked across the worn linoleum to the kitchen sink. There was a coffee cup still half full sitting on the counter and an empty crème brûlée dish in the sink.

"Well, at least she sweetened herself up," I said, reaching for the coffee mug. It was lukewarm to the touch—maybe half an hour old, given how warm the house was. You could grow orchids in here.

"Looks like the wicked witch decided to take her broom, buddy," I said. "Maybe when bridge is done for the day they can do an aerial show. Wouldn't that be fun?"

I laughed at my jokes but Keats didn't join in with his usual wide-mouthed grin. Instead, his muzzle turned left and right and his tail drifted slowly down.

"Okay, let's check the basement and yard before we head back. Honestly, if she's hoofing it and wasting my time, I'm going to be annoyed. She doesn't even have a cell so that I can call her."

Keats did a cursory circuit before leading me back to the golf cart. He knew Edna wasn't down for the count nearby and I trusted him.

"I'll catch up with her on the road, I bet." I pressed the pedal hard till I remembered the nails and slowed down. The cart could hit 30 miles per hour and it really did feel like a magic carpet on the gravel after the bumpy shortcut over.

I figured Edna must have gotten a good head start—or headed

onto one of the many side trails herself—because there was no sign of her. We rounded the curve that hid the marshy waterhole from view. That's how we happened to be so close when I finally saw Edna's black Mary Janes.

They weren't kicking up dust as she strode toward the farm. Instead, they were splayed in a most unladylike pose as she lay face down, practically submerged in Wilma's pig pool.

CHAPTER SIX

"Jilly, it's me." I paced up and down the lane with the phone to my ear as Keats did his due diligence.

"I don't need Keats' psychic abilities to know that," she said, over the clatter of pots. "Call display does the trick. What's taking you so long?"

"Edna's been... detained."

"Detained? She wanted to be here early to lord her hosting prowess over the breakfast table."

"Yes, well, she got a head start, no doubt to do just that. But then she was..."

"Detained?" Jilly supplied.

"Yes, detained. Permanently."

The clatter stopped abruptly and all I could hear was Jilly breathing hard as she absorbed my meaning, denied it briefly and then forged on. "Are you saying she..."

Her voice trailed off.

"Flew the coop. Gained her heavenly wings." I sighed. "Yes. Even if it looks quite the opposite from here."

"Where exactly is 'here'? Are you in her house?"

"No. She was on her way before I even got here but she was

apparently rudely interrupted by the pig pool. You know, the marshy spot where Wilma rolled me."

"Rudely interrupted?" I could tell Jilly was breathing in through her nose and trying to puff out her diaphragm, to ward off either hysteria or hysterical laughter. "Who interrupted her?"

"I think it may have been a 'what,'" I said. "That's what I need you to find out. Can you run down to the barn for me? Without letting any of the Bridge Buddies know something is amiss?"

"Of course." I heard the back door slam. "Half of them are still in bed and the other half are playing a warm up hand." She puffed slightly as she took the word "run" literally. "What am I looking for?"

"Just do a quick circuit and tell me if any of the critters are missing. Charlie will be in by nine, so all I did was take care of the chickens before heading over. I didn't even poke my head into the barn for fear of getting everyone going."

She counted off the animals as she went. "Alpaca, present. Two llamas, check and check. Two donkeys accounted for."

"So far, so good. Cows?"

"I'm inside the barn now. Heidi and Clara are peacefully chewing hay and Archie is just being adorable." There was a pause as she counted. "Six sheep in their pen. Eight goats in theirs. Florence just nipped my shoulder. Thanks for that, sweetheart." Another long pause followed and then, "Oh no."

I let out the breath it had felt like I'd been holding since I saw the prints in the silty mud beside the marsh. "Wilma?"

"Gone." The word was a grunt, as if she had bent over. "The lock's broken."

"Broken... or snapped?"

"Snapped. It looks like someone let her out deliberately. Are you saying she ran into Edna and took her down?"

"Can't tell for sure. All I know is that there are signs Wilma visited her favorite watering hole and that Edna is here now, too. Alone."

"Was she... was she maimed?"

"No, just drowned." I shook my head. "As if 'just drowned' is any better. Wilma is quite capable of a simple death roll, as you know."

"Edna probably aggravated her. She was as mean as a sow to you last night."

"True, but that doesn't mean my sow gets to drown her."

"I know. It's just that..."

"The crap is going to hit my reputation. Again. Silly city slicker Ivy Galloway can't keep her rescue animals locked down." I pressed my free hand against my forehead. "The Bridge Buddies are going to have a field day. They're the most influential women in town."

"Well, we don't know exactly what happened yet," Jilly said. "Maybe Edna had a heart attack in the wrong place. She was certainly stressed enough yesterday. You've called Kellan?"

"Yes. I called him first this time. Aren't you proud?"

"I am. Love really can accomplish miracles."

Heat rose in my cheeks. "This is professional."

"Oh, I know. And unfortunately Chief Hottie might find it hard to remember he loves you back for a while. But this too shall pass, Ivy. We'll get through it together."

"I hope so." The words came out like a shaky sigh. "Are you going to distract the guests with your magic mimosas?"

"I think cards are their drug of choice. All I need to do is feed them and herd them to their tables. Once they get going the house could blow down and they wouldn't notice. Sadly, no one will miss Edna till lunch."

"I miss her already," I said, and strangely, it was true. "There's a lot to be said for having a mean pig around to keep you on your toes."

"CALM DOWN AND tell me exactly what happened," Kellan said, as the ambulance drove away. They didn't bother with the siren because it was already too late: Edna had taken her final flight and parked her broom for good.

"I am calm," I said.

"Yeah? Then how come there's so much dust I can't breathe? Slow your pacing and talk to me. You're stressing Keats out."

That part was completely untrue. Keats enjoyed novelty and excitement. His ears and tail were up and his warm brown eye gleamed. That said, he wanted me to calm down and enjoy the hubbub with him. I couldn't do that. What I'd seen would join the growing collection of horrifying images compartmentalized in my unconscious to emerge in my sleep. I'd heard it wasn't good to repress these things, but what other option did I have if I wanted to keep going about my life as innkeeper and hobby farmer?

Sighing, I looked up at Kellan. He wasn't as excited as Keats, but he certainly looked animated. I supposed events like this posed an interesting puzzle for cops and acted like a jolt of caffeine.

"So, I came over to get Edna this morning and bring her back to the farm, as we'd agreed," I said.

"Why the golf cart?" he asked.

"Buttercup declined to serve," I said. "I guess she's not a morning car."

"Asher had that car serviced," he said. "How is it supposed to help if it won't run when you need it?"

"My point exactly. Buttercup belongs in a car museum, but Mom dinged her up too badly."

He frowned and then shook his head, as if reminding himself of the matter at hand. "So you took the golf cart?"

"Yeah, I wasn't in the mood for Edna's insults about my stick handling. She was on a tear last night after the Bridge Biddies battered her pride. I took the brunt of it."

He pulled out his notepad and started writing. "And you didn't see Edna's unfortunate plight on your way in?"

"I took the scenic route through the trails and came out right near the house, so I missed this." I gestured toward the pig pool. "I assume she'd already—uh—fallen by that point because her leg was... Well, you know. Like Lloyd Boyce's. And Wilf Darby's."

"Cold?" Kellan asked.

"Not quite. Not yet. But... lifeless, you know?" I thought about how her boney calf had felt through her support hose when I touched her with my index finger. "She was gone, and I knew it."

He nodded. "My forensics team will confirm time of death but I tend to agree with you."

"If I'd thought there was hope, I'd have tried CPR," I said. "I got certified every year at Flordale, in case Wilf had a heart attack, or caused one in his staff."

"At least you still have your sense of humor," he said. "I'm sure Edna died of natural causes in a most inopportune place. This swamp stinks like blazes."

"I know. I almost got my own wings here, remember?" I sighed again and met his dark blue eyes. "Kellan, there's something I need to tell you."

"Oh?" He was instantly on alert. "What's that?"

I beckoned and walked toward the swamp. "I had time to look around a bit and I found these prints."

"Footprints? Edna's?"

"Not exactly, although I did wonder if she hid cloven feet under those Mary Janes."

"Uh-oh." Kellan pulled out his phone and squatted beside the prints. Then he stood and stared at me. "And which barnyard beauty fits prints like that?"

"I would bet my next cup of coffee, which I desperately need, on my sly Cinderella Wilma."

"It couldn't be a wild boar? There are plenty around."

"Anything's possible. But Keats would be off in the bushes if there'd been wildlife around." I ran my hands through my hair and twisted it into a messy bun. "So I called Jilly and had her run down to the barn and check. Sure enough, Wilma's on the lam."

"Not again, Ivy. How did that happen?"

"Jilly said the lock was snapped. It looks like someone is targeting me all over again, Kellan. If Edna challenged Wilma to a duel she would have lost. I barely survived getting rolled in this swamp, as you know, and she's got nearly fifty years on me."

Now Kellan looked decidedly less animated. This was taking a turn he didn't like. I wasn't thrilled about it either. If my pig had drowned Edna Evans, I was in deep, dirty water, too.

Keats, on the other hand, was circling in ever widening loops looking for clues. Finally he came back to me and for once, his eerie blue eye looked puzzled.

"Keats smells something," I said.

"Of course he smells something. It's a fetid swamp."

"Yeah, but that's just business as usual. He smells something that confuses him, and he's not easily confused."

"What are you saying? This is no time to beat around the bush, Ivy. The team will be here in minutes to swarm the place."

My face suddenly grew hot and I struggled to pull in a breath. "Do you mind if I sit down?"

Kellan instantly put his arm around me and half-carried me to the golf cart. "Put your head between your knees if you feel faint."

"I don't feel faint, just sickened." I studied Keats for a moment as he resumed his investigation. "I think you're going to find that Edna didn't just conveniently die of natural causes face down in that swamp. Something happened."

"You think Wilma killed her?"

I shrugged. "Wilma is quite capable, and she was apparently available for the job." Then something struck me and I jumped out of the cart again. "Wait just one second." I walked to the side of the road. "See that?"

He peered at a small round circle beside a footprint. "Yeah?"

"That comes from Edna's walking stick. She hardly ever uses it, out of pride, but she probably needed something to lean on after yesterday's mean girl beatdown. But no matter how beleaguered she was, Edna would likely have fended Wilma off quite nicely with her cane. She's done it before, and like she told me only yesterday, she's a survivor."

"We'll look for the stick," he said, bending to take the sodden brown wool hat Keats managed to pull from the marsh while keeping his paws dry. "Whatever happened, natural or otherwise, it appears that Edna finally met something she couldn't survive."

CHAPTER SEVEN

I t was nearly noon before I got back to the farm and the family room was pretty much silent as I walked in, with everyone focusing intently on their game.

Clearing my throat, I said, "Folks, I'm afraid I have some bad news."

Eight sets of eyes rose, all somewhat dazed. Gertrude gave her head a little shake, either to dispel the fog or rebuke me. "We're in the middle of a game here, Ivy. What part of 'Do not disturb' don't you understand?"

"Like I said, I have bad news. Important news."

"More important than our bridge game?" Morag said. "The very reason we're paying top dollar to be here?"

They weren't paying top dollar at all. I'd given them a significant discount on my rates, both because I'd expected they'd be low maintenance and because any guest was a boon at this point. But no doubt they were paying top dollar to their bridge partners, which would make it an expensive vacation.

"I think it is more important, yes," I said. "How about I share it quickly and you can decide?"

I described what had happened to Edna briefly, mentioning

only her regrettable tumble into the swamp. There was no need to implicate Wilma until there was proof.

"Well," Gertrude said, blue eyes blinking rapidly. "That's a surprise."

"Completely unexpected," Joan said, her voice oddly dry.

"A terrible shame, the poor thing," Annamae said, groping in her blazer's breast pocket and pulling out an embroidered handkerchief.

"I always said nothing could kill Edna Evans," Morag said. She folded her large hands, and then refolded them in a new configuration. "I guess I was wrong."

The ringers murmured their sympathies, and Gertrude gave herself a little shake, like a dog coming out of a bath. "Edna is gone, apparently, and there is not a single thing we can do about it. So I suggest we play on."

"Gertrude," Annamae said. "We've just lost a longstanding member of our club. We can't just play on."

"It's what she would want, Annamae," Gertrude said. "Edna was nothing if not practical. We've lost plenty of members over the years, and that was Edna's own advice. Play on."

"I— I guess you're right," Annamae said. "We can talk about it later."

"Or not," Morag said. "It's unnerving losing a member just a bit older than me."

Jilly spoke at last. "I'll make something special in honor of Edna tonight and we can pay tribute to her."

"All right, that's settled," Gertrude said. "Now if you'll just deliver the lunch here, Jilly, we won't trouble you again till dinner."

The afternoon passed easily, as I spent most of it in the barn and fields with Charlie as a distraction. Wilma had returned on her own even before I did, demanding her breakfast. Charlie had replaced the lock with a stronger one and did the same with the henhouse. That lock had been tampered with too, after my morning rounds.

He let me work in silence for a while before saying, "Even if it was Wilma, it wasn't her fault. Someone let her out. And I know Edna well enough to think she probably threatened that pig, and possibly even hit her with her cane."

"Senna York said the same thing when I called." The vet, who was fast becoming a friend, was on her way over to examine Wilma. "I can't see a mark on her."

"She was her normal greedy grumpy self," Charlie said. "Not so different from Edna, if push came to pig."

"Charlie! That's terrible," I said, although it was no worse than what I'd been saying.

"Oh, come on, you know better than most how manipulative Edna could be. Tongue like a scythe."

"True that," I said, trailing after him as he checked every inch of fencing around the pastures. "I'm surprised I haven't bled out by now. But still. She didn't deserve to go that way."

He grunted agreement as he bent to tighten some wire with pliers. "No one deserves to land face down in a stinky swamp. But for now you need to focus on your guests. I'll stay late and come early till they're gone."

"Thanks, Charlie. I feel safer with you around."

He flashed me a glance with his twinkling blue eyes. "You could leave Keats down in the barn overnight. That's what farmers typically do, you know."

"Good idea," I said, smiling. "*Not*. That dog sleeps by my beside to keep the nightmares at bay. If I need to get a barn dog, I will."

Keats whined, as if letting me know that two dogs would be a crowd.

"Why didn't the barn camera work?" Charlie asked.

I shook my head. "I've got a tech guy coming around later, too.

I'm going to install so many cameras Florence won't be able to sneeze without my knowing about it."

"Great," Charlie said. "Remind me to wear a belt. I don't want your mother seeing any images of farmer's butt."

Squinting, I waited for him to meet my eyes. "We agreed never to discuss my mother."

"You agreed with yourself," he said. "I have no trouble discussing Dahlia. She's a lovely lady with a great sense of humor."

"Oh, she's a laugh all right," I said. "And on that note, I'll leave you to your work."

He chuckled. "Now I know how to get rid of you when you're in my way."

"The problem here is that you and I both know I would never fire you in a million years." I turned back on my way to the house. "Ask my mom how many times she's been fired, Charlie. Now, that's a funny story."

"It's a shame that employers don't appreciate her unique talents," he called after me. "And by the way, I got Buttercup purring like a kitten. You just need to know how to talk to her."

Great. Now I had another difficult animal on my hands.

JILLY OUTDID HERSELF WITH DINNER. There was a big tureen of Edna's favorite beef stew, another with grilled root vegetables, a basket of homemade biscuits and for dessert, a simple apple crumble pie. All of these had been on Edna's list of special requests in recent weeks. She preferred the harvest basics when all was said and done.

The Bridge Buddies were so quiet through the main course that I practically did conversational handsprings to break the silence. With 10 years of interviewing behind me in HR, I rarely had trouble getting people talking. But tonight, words were scarcer than hen's teeth until Jilly popped the cork on a bottle of champagne.

"Let's have a toast to Edna and say a few words," she said. "I'll go first, even though I only knew her for a couple of months." She cleared her throat. "I admire people who know what they want and persist despite obstacles. Edna Evans was certainly that. When she decided I'd cook for her, she made it happen, and I think she got me to check off every item on her wish list in record time, too."

"Here here," I said. "Edna had me wrapped around her finger and I don't quite know how she did that, because I was very much used to managing people. But she managed me, and I have to tip my hat to her."

Gertrude smiled. "That's because she scared the dickens out of you through school, Ivy. There's not a child from this town who doesn't have nightmares about vaccination day."

"I always planned my visits to Doc Grainer when Edna was on vacation," Joan said, with a laugh.

"Me too," Annamae said. "If it was urgent I drove over to Dorset Hills."

"Same," Morag said. "She ruled that doctor's office with an iron fist. It was her kingdom."

I raised my hand to stop the conversation from turning into a pile on. "She loved her career. She told me so only yesterday. Being independent was extremely important to her."

It was a subtle way of reminding them that Edna never had the same opportunities as the rest of them, being married to successful men. Gertrude's mouth snapped shut and of course, the others followed suit.

Finally Annamae dared to speak. "Women didn't usually get to have careers in our day. Sometimes I envy you girls."

"I know how hard it was even in my mom's era," I said. "She was only ever hired if there wasn't a man to do the job."

"That wasn't Dahlia's only challenge," Gertrude muttered.

"Oh, I know that." I gave her a sweet smile. "I'm just saying that Edna's accomplishments in supporting herself and buying a home were quite remarkable for the time."

"Granted," Gertrude said. "She had a rough start in life, too, yet I never heard a word of complaint about it."

"What happened?" I asked.

Gertrude shrugged. "Never got a straight answer out of her. All I know is that her family lived pretty much isolated out in the bush and a terrible fire claimed them all. Edna was the only survivor. She was on her own by age 15, and boarded in town till she could finish her schooling."

"And then there was the terrible heartbreak," Annamae said, tearing up again. "Everyone thought Merle Randall worshipped the ground she walked on, but then he suddenly broke things off. Edna was never the same after that. She got cold and mean."

"What happened to Merle after that?" I asked.

"Married and still running a pharmacy in Dorset Hills, as far as I know," Annamae said. "He did all right for himself."

"Poor Edna," I said. "She had a tough go of things."

Morag eyed Gertrude before saying, "We all make our choices, Ivy. Life deals out some manure to all of us, and we decide how to handle it. You know that as well as anyone here."

"True," I said. "But—"

"But Edna decided to terrorize children, including mine. Maybe especially mine." She sighed and looked around the table. "Maybe I should have let her win more."

"I always wondered that myself," Joan said. "My kids used to prank her all the time and I turned a blind eye."

"Mine too," Annamae said. "I tried to stop them but they just got sneakier."

"It's not our fault we played a better game than Edna Evans," Gertrude said. "I, for one, never let someone win just to be nice.

She didn't have the chops and we only kept her in the club because she took care of all the admin."

"You had advantages," I said, glancing at their hired partners, all of whom were eating without saying a word. I assumed that silence was part of the contract. Either that, or they were rightly terrified of the backlash the wrong comment could cause.

Gertrude held up her hand. "Stop right there. These so-called advantages are relatively recent. I could kick Edna's butt at cards fifty years ago, blindfolded."

"Bridge wasn't her gift," Annamae said. "No matter how clever she was in other ways."

"We just couldn't get her to leave," Morag said. "And we tried for decades."

The champagne was loosening their tongues and making them speak out of order. Jilly opened another bottle in the kitchen and refilled their flutes.

"That must have been hard for her," I said. "To know she wasn't wanted."

Gertrude raised her hand again. "Edna said you were soft, Ivy. You've got to realize this is farm country. People need to be tough to survive out here, even now. Edna knew that and she *was* tough. She got back at us in dozens of petty ways."

"I think she stole my cat," Morag said. "I didn't really care for it, but still. Who does that?"

"Mine too!" Annamae said. "One day she came over to drop off a new blazer and I never saw Fleecy again. A pure white cat is a rarity in these parts."

"Why on earth would she steal your cats?" I asked. "It must be a coincidence."

"A coincidence doesn't happen three times in the space of two months," Gertrude said. "I was afraid to replace mine in case it happened again. She was one heck of a mouser, too."

"It must have been a coyote," I said. "Edna despised pets of all kinds. She told me so."

Morag shrugged. "She despised us more."

"I worried so much about Fleecy," Annamae said, dabbing her eyes again. "Edna had access to medical supplies, you know. What if she used our cats in experiments?"

"After terrorizing our kids, I wouldn't put it past her," Gertrude said. After a moment, she added, "You don't think she...?"

"Made her own appointment to meet her maker?" Morag asked. "It's definitely crossed my mind."

"I don't believe that for one second," Joan said. "Edna had the means to orchestrate a comfortable demise in her canopied bed had she been so inclined. She would never have gone down in a fetid swamp by choice."

"I'm glad I didn't make a fuss about that hair appointment," Annamae said. "Even though it was wasted."

"Not wasted at all," Gertrude said. "You can't hold a good perm down. They'll fix things up nicely in the funeral home."

"That's right," Annamae said, brightening. "And I still have time to get my own hair done properly before then."

"I already notified Robbi," Gertrude said. "She's booking us in."

I pushed my seat back and rose. "Ladies. How about we adjourn and you can enjoy your apple pie over another game?"

They were up and away so fast their younger bridge stunt doubles couldn't begin to keep up.

CHAPTER EIGHT

I t felt like I'd only been asleep for minutes when I awoke at two a.m. to find Keats upright and staring at me. I could hear him panting, although it was cool enough in my bedroom.

"What's wrong, buddy?" I asked. "Are you feeling sick? Did Jilly slip you too much beef stew? Don't think I don't know about your little arrangement."

I flipped on the light and his tail came up immediately. Definitely not sick. He had something on his mind.

I did, too. The conversation at dinner had buffeted me around like the winds of a hill country winter. Edna had come off as unhinged, which I'd often felt myself, but now I could see how she turned out that way. She'd lost her family and the love of her life, only to be shut out for decades by mean girls. These four weren't the only ones, either: the club had a robust membership over the years, but they'd disappeared one by one. Younger people hadn't stepped in to replace them, as they had in many longstanding Clover Grove institutions. No doubt the club's reputation for petty bullying dimmed its appeal. Mom had been complaining about them since I was a kid.

Sitting up, I swung my legs over the side of the bed and Keats immediately started prancing. He had somewhere he wanted to go. My first thought was that someone was vandalizing the barn again, but if that were the case, he wouldn't be wagging his tail like this was our best adventure yet.

"Fine," I said. "I think I know what you want, and far be it from me to deny my best buddy anything his heart desires."

Slipping into my overalls and a fleece hoodie, I crept through the silent house after Keats. He knew the old, squeaky floorboards to avoid and it wasn't long before we were jogging toward the barn.

"This is reckless, Keats," I said. "The kind of thing that always bites us in the butt."

He circled me and dove at the back of my legs.

"Do NOT herd me. We've had this talk. I am not your live-stock." I unlocked the door to the shed. "Name another owner who'd take you on a fool's errand in the middle of the night."

He leapt onto the passenger seat of the golf cart and I pulled out slowly, keeping the lights out until we were far down the lane and somehow evading the worst potholes by memory. I didn't dare use the bumpy trails at that hour, so I took my chances on the highway shoulder. It wasn't far to Edna's driveway and luckily we didn't see a single vehicle. Keats braced himself on the dash, and the cold autumn wind blew back his ears and my hair. No doubt we looked crazy, but I felt strangely alive. Being trapped in my house with those women had starved me of oxygen. Now I had all I needed.

When we pulled up outside Edna's, Keats hopped out and circled me, careful to avoid any sudden lunges that might trip me. Using my phone light, I went straight to the pot of chrysanthemums under her front window and tipped it to get the key. She'd given me access about a week ago so that I could drop off food at my convenience.

I took the liberty now of letting myself inside.

"We missed something earlier, didn't we?" I said. "It feels like we have unfinished business."

Keats mumbled his agreement.

"We were here every day, sometimes twice a day. Edna was healthy and she had something to live for, namely making my life miserable. I highly doubt she'd make herself a coffee and polish off a crème brûlée if she felt ill or planned to off herself, am I right? Not the Edna we knew."

Keats mumbled further endorsement, which made me feel quite a bit better about basically breaking into Edna's house at two thirty in the morning.

"The problem is that the police have already combed the place," I said, pulling woolen gloves out of the pockets of my down jacket before unlocking the door. "What's left for us to find?"

Inside, we walked from room to room without much caution about my flashlight. With the thick brush all around, Edna's house was only visible from mine, and everyone at the inn was sound asleep.

I checked the kitchen and found the counter and sink empty, as expected. Kellan's team would have collected everything just in case the autopsy revealed that something other than natural causes had claimed Edna.

For some reason, I suspected that would prove to be the case. Maybe it was all the animosity among her so-called friends, or maybe it was some sort of misplaced loyalty. I owed Edna nothing really, and yet I wanted to make sure she got a fair deal, at least in death.

"Oh Keats, I can't," I said, as we neared the master bedroom door. "Those dolls were creepy enough in daylight. Now they're..." I directed the light at the row of girls. "Demonic."

Oddly, facing Lloyd Boyce's snakes had been easier, and that was really saying something.

I tried to walk away but my black-and-white sidekick nudged me forward gently.

The police hadn't taken the dolls, so I stepped into the room to take a closer look. There were a dozen, at least. Blonde ones, redheads, brunettes, and even one with short white-blonde curly hair, that resembled Edna's perm. The perm doll was smaller than the rest, yet tucked behind the others, as if to protect her from the bullies of life.

Pulling out the little perm girl, I examined her closely and then held her out to Keats. "Anything we need to worry about here?"

His pant sounded like a yes-yes-yes.

I set the doll on the bed so that I could take off her dress. With woolen gloves, it was challenging.

All of sudden a voice rang out in the darkness. "Hello!"

I dropped the doll with a little scream, grabbed the light and spun around. Keats wasn't fazed at all. In fact, his mouth hung open in his sloppy grin. Laughing at me.

"Oh gees," I said, realizing what had happened. "It's the doll talking. Duh."

Turning back, I picked her up. This time she said, "Don't be sad."

"I'll be sad if I want to," I said. "You do you."

"You're pretty," she said.

Keats mumbled something that sounded disparaging. "I *am* pretty for three in the morning," I said.

"What a nice day," the doll said.

"That's enough out of you, young lady. What else are you hiding?"

I turned her upside down and gave her a shake. She let out a wail that was understandable given the circumstances. But I didn't need to hear the rattle to know it was there.

"I am so sorry to do this to you, baby girl, but you've given me no choice."

Twisting hard to the left, I pulled her head off. A tiny key fell onto the floral bedspread. I immediately put her head back on, dressed her, and tucked her back behind the others. It felt like a desecration of what seemed like Edna's private nursery. Maybe these represented all the children she wished she'd had. Or all the children she wished she'd been kinder to, in her school nurse days.

"Mission half accomplished, Keats. A tiny key like this could fit a jewel box, or a diary. Honestly, Edna didn't seem like the type for either. I only saw her wearing a watch."

I shone the light around the room, looking for obvious fits for the key. But I couldn't justify going through Edna's drawers or cupboards. At the moment, her death looked either natural or accidental, and at 80 it was a reasonable assumption. Keats and I just happened to sense there was more to the story. While I didn't always trust my own intuition, I did trust my dog's. For the moment, I would put this key in my pocket for safekeeping and either let Kellan deal with it later or replace it before Edna's executor took over the estate.

Back in the living room, I perched on the puffy chair closest to the window. Staring toward my property, I thought about Edna whiling away all those hours watching life unfold at Runaway Farm. She must have been very lonely. And yes, her experiences had made her mean but my mind kept circling back to the expression, "hurt people hurt people." I'd seen it over and over in my HR career as I counselled people on workplace issues or family problems. Aside from a small number of born sociopaths, I believed most troubled people became that way because of isolation or abuse, and the fear, anger and loneliness that inevitably followed.

"Lately it seemed like she was mellowing a bit," I told Keats now. "Who knows what might have happened had she lived a little longer and been seduced by our charms and Jilly's cooking?"

He tilted his head, staring at me in much the same way Jilly did when I was taking things too far.

"Okay, whatever. I just feel bad for her. Is that so wrong? Don't you start calling me soft, too."

I was surprised at the sadness welling up and threatening to bring tears along for the ride. Edna was a thorn in my side, but I had come to enjoy our frequent visits. Well, almost. Sometimes I wondered if her jabs were meant to toughen me up for a rough ride. Either way, there was going to be a vacuum in my world that wouldn't be easily filled. Good frenemies were hard to find.

"I really hope she wasn't crushed under Wilma, Keats. That would be the last and worst indignity." I leaned back in the chair. "Not to mention a big problem for Wilma and me."

Sighing, I turned to the old oak trunk where Edna stored her spyware. Normally the binoculars were within easy reach under the curtains but she'd put them away. I lifted the lid and pulled out the night vision goggles that had at first appalled me, then proven instrumental in solving the most recent murder at my farm.

Keats started to pace and before long his panting accelerated past yes-yes-yes to no-no-no. He was done here and had no patience for sentimentality.

"We'll go soon," I said. "Let's just take a look at the world through Edna's eyes." I directed the goggles toward my farm. "It's a daunting prospect but I think I can handle it."

I expected to see nothing. Only the llamas, alpaca and donkeys stayed out at night.

What I saw, however, made me jump to my feet. There was a light bobbing around the barn, moving steadily toward the henhouse. I couldn't make out anything except the fact that the person with the light seemed to wobble a little as if he or she were drunk.

Maybe one of the Bridge Buddies, or their paid partners, had discovered the tangerine vodka I bought for Edna sitting on the kitchen counter.

But there was no way I wanted anyone—drunk or otherwise—messing with my livestock.

"Come on, Keats," I said, replacing the goggles quickly, and running to the front door. "I'm going to kick some intruder butt. And you'd better be ready with your signature ear-ripper maneuver, because I want to make sure this fox never visits my henhouse again."

CHAPTER NINE

Buttercup purred like the kitten Charlie had likened her to as I drove into town the next morning with Jilly riding shotgun. Our guests were fed, settled and intent on their game. The house could have fallen around them and they wouldn't notice our brief absence. Charlie was just a shout away if they needed anything.

Jilly turned to stare at the side of my head. Somehow that look felt different in Mom's jalopy than it did in my big truck. I was at a distinct disadvantage. Yellow had never been my color.

"So after you careened back over the rough trails from your dangerous mission, no one was even there?" She cleared her throat. "I mean, I'm glad no one was there. I'm just trying to get the facts straight."

"It wasn't that dangerous." I waved my right hand. It was rather nice not to be clutching the gearshift all the time. Freeing. "Aside from the trail, of course. I had no reason to think anyone would be lurking around Edna's house and she gave me permission to use the key."

"Yet you've already stated for the record that your 'spidey sense' was firing and you wondered if Edna had run into a tougher adversary than Wilma."

"We can't give much credence to my spidey sense, can we? If it worked properly, I wouldn't have so many close calls."

"Exactly!" Jilly was triumphant. "You trusted your intuition that trouble was looming and ran straight into its cold embrace."

I glanced over my shoulder. "You have a rival poet, Keats."

"I'm not joking, Ivy. I mean, I am but I'm not. You saw someone poking around near the barn and you didn't call me, let alone Kellan. You tried to confront an intruder on your own."

"Not on my own. With Keats. You don't think he can take down a drunken senior? That's child's play to a dog like him. Besides, he let me know that the coast was clear as soon as we got back. It was a bust."

Keats rested a paw on Jilly's shoulder and licked her ear.

"Do not sweet talk me, mister," she said, flicking off his paw. "No more stew for you if you're going to let Ivy run off on hare-brained schemes."

"It was his idea," I said, throwing him to the proverbial dogs. "I was sound asleep and he stared me awake. He wanted to get going."

"Keats always wants to get going. That's a given. But last I checked, you're the one in the driver's seat of this relationship and you could just say no to middle-of-the-night excursions on a dog's whim."

"True, but we did actually find something, remember?"

"A key to Edna's teenage diary by the looks of it," she said. "I'm quite sure she wouldn't want you poking around her house and snapping heads off her treasured doll collection."

I sank a little behind the wheel. "I'm not proud of that. Those dolls seemed like her babies."

Jilly finally deflated a little. "I know Edna's death hit you hard, Ivy. I'm not sure why, considering how poorly she treated you, but I can see that it did. Sadly, you may be the only one who truly cares about her passing. The bridge ladies didn't have a single nice thing to say about her and now they're all fussing about getting their hair done for her funeral. Hypocrites."

"The pillars of our community," I said. "What a shame that they have the power to bring us business or chase it away. I'd like to stay on their good side, so I won't ask who was tottering around the barn last night."

"Kellan can do it. You wouldn't get a straight answer and it might not be them anyway." Jilly let Keats slink through the seats and into her lap. He had her wrapped up pretty tight these days. "Someone sprinkled nails on Edna's driveway. Maybe it's a local teen pulling pranks."

"Possibly. I'm just sorry I didn't get back home in time to see for myself. I should have taken the highway. It would have been faster than the twisty trail."

"And safer," Jilly said.

"On that we agree," I said, hoping to make peace with her before we arrived for the meeting.

After a few moments of more cordial silence, she asked, "Remind me why we're going to Daisy's?"

"Because all of our family meetings are at Daisy's. As the eldest, it gives these events a certain gravitas."

She laughed. "I mean why are we going *together*? I'm not part of the family, in case you hadn't noticed."

"You *are* my family, in case you hadn't noticed. The rest of them are just my childhood roommates."

Jilly laughed again. I was gaining ground. "Don't you think it will be awkward?" she asked.

I turned into Daisy's neighborhood on the far side of Clover Grove. "Oh, it'll be awkward, all right. These meetings always are. We should have brought the vodka."

"It's 10 a.m."

"Trust me, you'll wish you had some when Mom gets going.

I'm hoping she'll rein things in a little with you present. Heaven only knows what she's done this time."

"So now the word 'buffer' is in my job description, too."

"You wear many hats, Jilly Blackwood," I said, laughing. "One day I hope your job description will include 'sister-in-law' and this suffering will be legitimately yours to share."

She shook her head. "Asher and I still haven't had a proper date, so it might be a little early to talk about my becoming a charter member of the Galloway clan."

"Yeah, remind me to give you a night off for the induction ceremony."

"Sounds inviting, but our schedules never seem to sync up."

"Oh, they could sync up just fine if you wanted them to, Jilly. You're riding the brakes."

I was riding Buttercup's brakes, too. The car was playing fast and loose with the rules of the road. No wonder Mom struggled with stop signs. This old girl was a bronco who required force, as well as finesse.

"Maybe I am a little," Jilly admitted eventually. "My intuition says the timing isn't quite right for us."

"Your intuition? Is that something like spidey sense? Which you've just told me not to trust?"

She turned to shoot me a glare. "Very funny. Romance and reckless behavior are two different things."

"Since when?" I pulled up in front of the house and took a stab at parallel parking. Without power steering and brakes, it was like maneuvering a yacht. "Both can be dangerous."

"I suppose we're speaking of Chief Hottie, now," she said.

"In our case, he's the one riding the brakes. I'd free up some time in my schedule pretty darned fast if he invited me on a real date."

"We've already established that you're a risk-taker."

"You've notched up plenty of points for courage lately, my

friend." I pulled the car out again and tried some new moves. "Come on, sweetheart. You can do this."

"All right," Jilly said, sighing. "I'll say yes the next time Asher asks me."

"Perfect. I meant Buttercup but that worked out well. And there's no time like the present, because here he comes now."

I jumped out of the car, leaving it running. "You want me to drive that thing, you can play valet," I said.

"You got it." He was grinning from ear to ear as he noticed Jilly had stayed inside.

Grabbing his arm, I said, "Be good to my friend, okay?"

He nodded before squeezing behind the wheel. "I got this, sis."

I WALKED into Daisy's kitchen with only my canine backup, since Jilly was canoodling in Buttercup.

Everyone except Asher has assumed normal positions. Daisy wandered around with a spray bottle of cleanser and a cloth, wiping down anything anyone touched. Mom sat on a stool that was far too high for her, pumps swinging and clacking against the metal legs. Iris sat with legs crossed and arms folded at the kitchen table, the elegant opposite to Poppy, slouched beside her. Poppy's hair had been red the last time I saw her but today it was an interesting shade of gunmetal blue. Meanwhile, genial Violet wandered from place to place trying to soothe everyone's frayed nerves when hers were likely the most frayed of all.

Asher came in holding Jilly's hand. Her face looked like the middle name all the Galloway women shared: Rose.

"Jilly, darling, come for a hug," Mom said. "If I get down from here, I may never get back up. Why do you insist on such high stools, Daisy?"

"Because I have five men in the house over six feet tall," Daisy said. "You could sit at the table, Mom."

"And miss towering over all of you? Never." She leaned over and gave Jilly a hug, allowing my friend to prop her up before she slid off. The red satiny skirt Mom was wearing was just a bad call all around.

"Jilly and I are on the clock," I said. "So let's get to the good stuff. What's Mom done now?"

My mother smirked. "Darling, take my stool. This time the hot seat is yours."

"Mine! What did I do?"

"Daisy has been elected spokesperson." Mom spun back and forth on the stool to watch everyone's expressions. That was going to end badly, if she didn't mind her satin.

"Then let me speak, Mom," Daisy said. Her face twitched from the burden of delivering the message they'd developed together before I arrived.

Everyone fell silent and my eyes jumped from her face to Asher's. Normally he was all smiles, but today, despite making headway with Jilly, he looked more solemn than I thought possible.

I looked around for Keats and found him already sitting on my feet. He knew I was in trouble before I did.

"Daisy, just get it over with," I said. "I can take it."

She sucked in a deep breath and blurted, "We want you to sell the farm."

"Sell the farm! Are you kidding me? This farm is the best thing that ever happened to me."

"You've almost been killed twice and now you're in trouble again."

"Who says I'm in trouble again?" I turned to my brother. "Asher, what gives?"

"Edna Evans," he said, shrugging. "She got a bad egg."

"Could you be more specific?" I asked.

"Not without aggravating my boss." He grinned sheepishly. "I've already said more than he wanted."

"Are you NOT saying that Edna was poisoned?"

He nodded. "That's exactly what I'm not saying."

"But what does that have to do with me?"

"You served the poison."

Jilly gasped and walked away from him to stand beside me. "The monogrammed crème brûlée. Made with Edna's own eggs."

"How tragic," Mom said. "You baked this toxic dessert, Jilly? Or was Mandy McCain responsible?"

"Mandy made and decorated them." Jilly's voice faded to a whisper. "But they were under my care all day." Her voice was a mere peep when she added, "No one else got sick."

"You did nothing wrong," I said. "Obviously someone spiked Edna's portion. One of the guests, I presume."

Asher sliced his finger across his throat. "No speculation, no discussion. Chief's orders."

I stood to my full height and straightened my shoulders. "One of my guests was poisoned, Asher. I'll be speculating all right."

"Then speculate silently." He nodded at Mom. "Please."

"I'm not the squeaky wheel in this family," she said. "Or at least, not the loudest. I managed to keep my dating life a secret for quite some time, didn't I?"

"If only that silence had lasted forever," Poppy said. "We all needed family counselling after that disclosure."

Daisy raised a hand. "We're going off topic, here. The point of this meeting was to share our safety concerns with Ivy."

"Right," Poppy said. "Short story: you need to get out of farming, Ivy. It's bad for you, it's bad for us."

"How exactly is my hobby farm bad for you?" I turned on Poppy and she gave me a cheeky smile. She wasn't afraid to get right up in your face, which made it easier to be direct. With the rest of the Galloway women, it was often a subtle dance.

Poppy flipped her gunmetal hair. "It's called the butterfly effect. Something happens to you and it makes waves for all of us. Now we're the family of someone with a big problem."

"Ivy, I'm afraid Poppy's right this time," Mom said. "It's one murder after another on that farm. It's just not sustainable."

I stared around at them, stunned. My fingertips and toes felt numb as blood rushed away to where it was needed more—my vital organs, and apparently my face, which grew hot. Keats shifted right onto my feet and whined. "It's okay, buddy," I said. My voice didn't even sound like mine. It was a harsh croak.

"Ivy, don't take this so hard," Daisy said. Her hazel eyes, like mine only darker, filled with sympathy. "It's just that we're all so worried. You've been lucky before, but it feels like only a matter of time before..."

"The grim reaper catches up with me?" I asked. "Or one of you?"

Daisy's gaze dropped to an invisible fleck on the counter and she started scrubbing. "Something like that. I have kids to worry about."

Asher pushed himself off the fridge. "On the bright side, the actual death happened on Edna's property. But we have to assume it was meant to happen on yours. And you've said someone's been creeping around."

"And darling, what about Kellan?" Mom asked, nearly sliding off the stool as she turned again. This time, Jilly didn't help and Mom tilted like a boat taking on water. Any other day, it would have been amusing.

"What about him?" I said.

"Well, you can't expect the chief to commit to someone with so much baggage," she said, clawing her way upright. "Men want easy-breezy women who make their lives easier, not harder. Worrying about your safety is a distraction from his job. The Chief of Police can't afford distractions."

Clenching my hands into fists, I felt the tingling recede. This wasn't the first time I'd felt under attack. Not by a long shot. It was just the first time I felt like my entire family had turned against me at once. Jilly crowded a little closer and squeezed my left fist. I couldn't count the times she'd infused me with courage in my corporate career, just as she did now. Thankfully, the old Ivy surfaced exactly when I needed her. Calm, confident and capable of diffusing conflict.

"I'm sorry you feel so anxious about what's been happening at Runaway Farm, everyone." My voice was strong. Keats got off my feet and Jilly's hand rose to my sleeve, ready to shut me down with a sharp tug. "Now that I understand your point of view I'll most certainly take that into consideration going forward. As you can imagine, I see things differently. I've committed to the farm and the animals in my charge. What's more, I love the place and the job in a way I never could have imagined." I scanned their faces in a cool, detached way as if they were members of a hostile audience. I'd faced plenty of those before. "But here's the thing: I believe Keats, Jilly and I did good work for this community in helping to bring Lloyd Boyce's killer to justice. We did it again when someone chose my farm to dispatch Wilf Darby. And now it looks like I've been innocently drawn into trouble over Edna Evans. Am I going to stand down from that trouble? Probably not. But I will take what you've said under serious advisement."

Poppy raised her hands and gave a slow clap. "Woo. Nice speech, sis."

I offered a stiff corporate smile, still so familiar and surprisingly comforting. "Now, if you don't mind, Jilly and I have an inn to run."

Asher tried to catch Jilly's hand on the way out and she jerked it away. The gesture may have packed the biggest punch of all: my best friend was willing to forfeit her future happiness to support me. That wasn't right, and I had some serious thinking to do about it. In the moment, however, it felt like gold.

Keats stayed in the back seat on the way home so that he could rest his head on my shoulder and mumble support into my ear. Jilly let him work his magic and when she felt a shift, spoke up. "Don't take it so hard, Ivy. They're just your childhood roommates, remember? Keats and I are your family now."

It was exactly the right thing to say and I smiled in spite of myself. "I may not say this often enough, Jilly Blackwood, but I love you."

She laughed. "Actually, you've never said that."

"Well, I couldn't maintain a killer reputation and be dropping L-bombs around like candy." My phone buzzed in my bag at Jilly's feet. "Can you get that? I worry about the Bridge Buddies adding to the pile of victims."

She pulled out the phone and stared at it. "It's a text from Cori Hogan. She wants to meet with you."

"Uh-oh. That can't be good." Cori was part of a band of renegade dog rescuers in our neighboring town of Dorset Hills, who called themselves the Rescue Mafia. Hannah Pemberton had been a key part of their team, but after she left they avoided the farm because of the frequent police presence. Their strategies for protecting animals were always creative, and seldom legal. "I can't very well say no."

Jilly shook her head. "Better you than me."

"I take back my L-bomb," I said, as the phone buzzed again.

Checking the phone, she mumbled something under her breath before reading aloud, "Bring Jilly and Keats."

CHAPTER TEN

C harlie wasn't thrilled when I asked him to leave the barn to see to any hospitality needs of the Bridge Buddies. He'd known them all his life and had no problem at all saying he was terrified. But he agreed to go inside when he heard about my summons from Cori Hogan. Years ago, he'd been part of the Rescue Mafia, too. He still helped on occasion, despite "aging out," as he put it.

I didn't know how big the core rescue group actually was, but they had networks of supporters throughout all of hill country. Today, only four women had gathered around a huge bronze chow chow on the outskirts of Dorset Hills. Unlike the rest of the city's many dog statues, the chow sat on its own, surrounded by bush at the base of an old trail that wasn't maintained. That made it a good meeting place for the renegades.

I don't know what I'd expected, but they looked like regular people. In fact, they were all attractive, even the tough dog trainer, Cori. She was petite and fit, with short glossy brown hair and dark eyes. Like her friends, she was dressed in black, as if ready to leap into action at a second's notice. Unlike her friends, she wore black wool gloves with orange middle fingers. I suspected these were her trademark, and instantly admired her sense of humor.

I knew them by sight from the online TV show, The Princess and the Pig, which had chronicled Hannah Pemberton's life at the farm. Cori and Bridget Linsmore, the leaders of the group, stepped forward and made the formal introductions. The other two women were Remi Malone, who was clutching a beagle, and Andrea MacDuff, a beauty with auburn hair.

"I'm sorry we haven't been out to the farm since you took over," Bridget said. She was tall and fair, the opposite of Cori, and an elegant, feathered black dog stuck close to her side. "We've been away a lot on Dog Town business, and now I'm doubling down to prepare for my Thanksgiving Rescue Pageant."

I waved away her apology. "I completely understand, and really it's for the best," I said. "Things have been a little... unsettled since I arrived."

"Murder can do that," Cori said, grinning. "What kind of weird karma did you bring with you from Boston?"

Keats left my side and sat in front of Cori. With any other dog, I'd say he was fawning. He was certainly agog with admiration of the tiny trainer. She glanced down at him and nodded, signifying some sort of tacit understanding. It made me suspect I wasn't the only one with a special conduit into the canine mind.

"No idea," I said. "I lived a life devoid of drama until just before I left the city. Boring, even. Right, Jilly?"

My friend looked like a deer in the headlights surrounded by these rescue warriors, but she managed a nod. "Boring. Both of us."

"Not anymore," Cori said.

"It's like I'm making up for lost time," I said. "There's never a dull moment now."

"Yeah, about that... This whole murder-at-the-farm thing?" Cori raised her hands and spun them till the orange flares dizzied me slightly. "It's just not sustainable, Ivy."

They were the exact words my mother had uttered earlier, and it was highly unlikely they'd had prior communication. My fingers and toes tingled, just as they had at the family meeting, only much worse. I was comfortable ignoring or even defying my family, but not the Rescue Mafia. Their opinion I cared about. I had no doubt they'd taken a vote to endorse Hannah's decision to put the farm in my hands. Now I feared I'd disappointed them all with what was just a streak of bad luck. At least, mostly. I wouldn't deny making a bad decision or five along the way, too.

Remi stepped forward, cradling a sweet-looking beagle in her arms like a baby. She'd come across as incredibly kind on Hannah's online show. The beagle, Leo, was supposedly one of the most loved dogs in all of Dorset Hills.

"What Cori is trying to say is that we're worried about you, Ivy," she said now.

"Worried about the animals, more like," Cori said. "We heard Wilma was initially—and unfairly—fingered for the death of Edna Evans."

I gasped. "How did you know?"

Cori waved a dismissive glove. "We know things. Edna Evans was a constant thorn in Hannah's side and really won't be missed."

"Cori!" Remi and Andrea offered a joint, scandalized protest.

"I say what we all think," Cori said. "That's my role. Anyway, I fully expect that Ivy's chief of police boyfriend will find out in due course that Edna was poisoned."

This time Jilly and I both gasped. "That's not public knowledge," I said.

Cori laughed. "Private knowledge is the only kind worth having. We stay connected."

"Well, the investigation has barely begun but obviously Wilma's name will be cleared."

"Good," Cori said. "She's one mean sow, and she probably wouldn't have thought twice about ending Edna, but we really don't want more bad press for Runaway Farm. We all worked very hard to salvage it."

I nodded. "I know. I've watched all the shows."

Bridget raised her hand to silence Cori. "Then you probably understand that we mean well when we ask if you'd like to sell Runaway Farm, Ivy. Sometimes it seems like the place is cursed. So many things have gone wrong there, and long before your time, I might add. But recent events have come hard and fast and it must be overwhelming."

"You could turn a very tidy profit and start an inn someplace safer," Andrea said. "I'm in real estate, so I'd help. With Hannah's blessing."

"We'd rehome the animals, of course," Cori said. "Making sure every last one of them was happy. Even Wilma."

Jilly clutched my sleeve again and Keats left Cori's side to sit by mine. That gave me the strength to ask, "Does Hannah *want* me to sell the farm? Are you saying she doesn't trust me anymore?"

"No," Remi said. Her voice was loud enough to startle Leo into sitting upright in her arms. "Hannah is worried about you, that's all. She's offered to hire a security detail but knows the police will take issue with that right now."

"Why hasn't she contacted me directly?" I asked.

"Because it broke her heart to leave that farm," Remi said. "It's painful for her to talk about, even to us. She wants you to live out the dream she had to forfeit for family."

"Well, she could have said no to her dad," Cori told Remi. "I would have."

"He's sick and he's the only parent she has left," Remi said. "We can't blame her and her brother for going, and she couldn't care for the farm properly from Europe."

"She should have left it with us," Cori said.

"We've all got targets on our backs as big as Ivy's," Bridget said. Her hand reached for the black dog's head and for a moment I envied her. The dog was so tall and so willing to be stroked. It wasn't easy to snatch a pat from Keats when you needed one. He was young and always on the move, not to mention considerably smaller.

I looked down at him now, feeling instantly guilty about my traitorous thoughts. He was staring back at me with his blue eye, no doubt reading my mind. But he wasn't one to hold a grudge. Instead, he gave my pant leg a rare lick as if to say, "Buck up, little camper."

So, I did. Just as I had earlier with my family, I straightened my shoulders. I was as tall as Bridget and towered over Cori. I also had something none of them had—a decade of faking it in the cutthroat corporate world. It was amazing what you came to appreciate about prison once you left it behind.

But that didn't mean I ever wanted to go back.

"Listen, ladies," I said.

"Do not call me lady." Cori's voice had a thunderous edge but I simply smiled. After all the fearsome executives I faced at Flordale, she couldn't scare me. Much.

"Okay, listen, worthy rescue renegades." I smiled to lighten the mood. "I appreciate your concern, and especially Hannah's. But Runaway Farm isn't just a job that I can give up. It's a calling." I glanced down at Keats again and he waved the white tuft of his tail. "I'd go so far as to say it's my destiny. I love every furry face in my custody. I've even rescued a couple of my own, you know."

"She isn't kidding," Jilly said. "I call it Ivy's Ark."

Cori raised one glove, which I matched with my own raised palm before continuing. "I enjoy running the inn, too. At least with Jilly's help." My friend squeezed my arm again and I finished my speech. "So, no. I'm not selling. And no, I won't be driven out by some bad luck. If you want to continue offering help now and then, I'd be glad to receive it. But I don't want you to put yourselves or your work in jeopardy. Because I know that's *your* calling."

Taking a step toward me, Cori stared up into my face. After a moment or two, she shrugged. "You know what? I like you, Ivy Galloway. And I don't like many people."

She spoke with the true confidence of knowing her opinion meant something. And judging by Keats' fanning tail, it truly did.

"Ain't that the truth," Remi muttered.

Cori turned on her. "People who persist in treating dogs like handbags forfeit the right to comment. Look at Ivy's dog, Remi. Independent, yet obedient. He has his own opinions."

"That he does," I said, laughing. "And he isn't afraid to share them."

"Not everyone can manage a border collie. Or even be managed by a border collie, which I think is more the case here," Cori said. "I doubt I could even steal him."

"Steal him!" I glanced quickly at Keats and his mouth hung open, as if enjoying the joke.

"Almost every dog transfers allegiance to Cori," Bridget said. "She has magic powers of canine seduction. Thank god Beau chose me over her."

"And Leo chose me," Remi said. "Even if he isn't Cori's superstar."

"He could be," Cori said. "If you ever let him walk on his own legs."

Bridget gave a sweeping wave to end the attack. "We've got to go. Mayoral business."

"It's always something," Cori grumbled. "Isla treats us like her own personal army."

"And we're happy to serve after what we went through with the last mayor," Bridget said.

As we walked back to the parking lot, Remi said, "I'm sorry if Cori upset you. We all mean well."

"I know." I reached out and touched Leo's long ears. They

were long and silky, and impossible to resist. "We share a common goal of keeping Runaway Farm safe."

Cori, who was at the front of the pack, waved a glove over her shoulder, directing the orange flare at Remi. "If I've worried you, Ivy, please accept Remi's apology."

Bridget shook her head, smiling. "What Cori means to say is that we are at your service. Solving murder isn't our area of expertise, but general security is. What we've learned about protecting dogs and each other can help."

"I don't want to draw you guys into my troubles," I said. "Like I said, you have your own calling in rescue."

"It's such fulfilling work," Remi said. "I wish you and Jilly could join us."

"Someday, I hope," I said.

Cori turned and gave me a grudging smile. "Your skills in the crime-solving arena could come in very handy. If you can manage to stay on the right side of the grass." Remi squeaked another protest but Cori forged on. "If anything happens to you—"

"It won't," Remi interrupted.

"But if it does," Cori continued, "I'll take Keats."

Jilly raised her hand now. "Get in line, lady. I'm his backup."

Keats danced around between us, utterly delighted to be the center of so much attention.

Cori flipped a glove at Jilly, and then added, "You're okay, too."

CHAPTER ELEVEN

The large parking area at Runaway Farm was almost full when we got back from our Rescue Mafia liaison. There were four police SUVs and a big truck with the Clover Grove coat of arms.

"What's going on?" Jilly said, craning to watch police officers as they carried boxes out the front door.

I didn't answer as I spun the wheel hard to squeeze Buttercup into a tight space. What was Kellan thinking by making me drive this old thing? Was it a joke? How were the good people of Clover Grove better off with Buttercup back on the road?

After a couple of tries, I got the car parked and then turned to Jilly and stopped her before she could get out. "I have bad news, my friend. Those officers are picking your kitchen bare."

Her sudden screech hurt my ears and sent Keats lunging into the rear footwell. "How dare they?"

"They're looking for whatever poisoned Edna, Jilly. You know they have to do that."

"It happened at Mandy's store, not in my kitchen," she said.

"I really hope that's true, but isn't there a chance that one of the Bridge Buddies slipped a little something under the E on Edna's dessert?"

Jilly groaned. "If it did happen under my watch, we'd never live it down. Five-star country cuisine that kills... I can see the reviews now."

My friend's gorgeous green eyes filled and spilled over. This felt like a complete and utter violation to her. It moved me that she felt so strongly about this place I'd just had to defend to doubters. Well, we'd show them. The three of us.

"Jilly, remember how you're always telling me we'll get through this together? Now it's my turn. We *will* get through this. I know that with every fiber of my being and Keats does, too. Look at him."

The distraction worked. She turned to see the dog back on the seat with his tail lashing. He gave her the full force of his sympathetic brown eye, and when that wasn't enough, poked his head through the seats to give her cheek a generous slurp.

"Ewww, Keats," she said. "You're not the smooching type."

"He is now. You fought a duel with Cori for him and won."

Shaking her head, she finally smiled. "You two are something else. Now maybe you can put your heads together and figure out how I'm going to feed ten of us when Mandy McCain's kitchen will likely be closed, too."

"I'll go into town right now and arrange for catering," I said.

"Give me a few minutes to think about my menu," she said. "I'll have time while you chat with Kellan."

"That can wait till I get back," I said, quickly. "The guests must eat."

She pointed and grinned before opening the car door. "Chief trumps chef."

KELLAN TURNED and leaned against the fence of the pasture that held the alpaca, llamas and donkeys. No matter where we started out or what path we took, that was always where we ended up. He probably thought he had a choice in the matter, but Keats was calling the shots. Maybe the dog hoped the sight of Alvina, the cavorting alpaca, would make Kellan go easy on me. It never worked but you couldn't blame a dog for trying.

"So let me get this right," he said, crossing his arms. "You got out of bed at two a.m. on the dog's whim and hurtled over to Edna's to have a poke around."

It wasn't a question so I didn't treat it as such. "We didn't *hurtle*. We kept a rather sedate pace on the only vehicle that seems to cooperate with me." He opened his mouth and I hastened to add, "Did you put me in Buttercup just for a laugh, by the way? She's already broken down once and steering a cruise liner would be easier."

He pressed his lips together to suppress a grin. It was nice seeing that it was harder for him to stay mad at me now. That was a significant advancement, or so I hoped.

"Don't change the subject," he said. "You broke into Edna's house. For what?"

"I'd tell you if I knew. It really was a whim, more or less. I felt like I'd missed something earlier. And I felt like I owed it to her to take a second look."

"There was no indication of foul play at that point," he said.

"I had a feeling," I said. "You saw the Bridge Buddies beating her down and it only got worse later. It wasn't a big stretch of the intuition to think someone took the bullying too far."

"Heaven forbid you trust me to do my job," he said, sliding a foot to the left.

Keats was pressing in on him with sheepdog body language and Kellan was responding completely unconsciously. At least there was no nipping of pant cuffs today, for which I was grateful.

That seemed to irk Kellan more than anything. He was always meticulously dressed, whether in uniform or civvies. No wonder he kept looking around at the farm and shaking his head. He probably wasn't aware of that either. The man was likely in constant conflict, feeling the pull of our high school romance while facing today's reality. I shrugged mentally. There was nothing I could do about his inner struggle. I'd committed to this place again twice today and my future was covered in so much fur it was ridiculous.

"I trust you," I said. "But it doesn't hurt to have a couple more sets of eyes on the situation, does it?"

"It may well have hurt you to have a set of night goggles on the situation, now, mightn't it? After you survived your hurtle back over rough trails, you could have been staring down the barrel of a gun, for example. That happens out here more than you know. Locals mistake people for bears."

"Seems like a stretch but we'll run with it," I said. "On the bright side, nothing happened. Keats sniffed around while I made sure the animals were locked down and the cameras were working. Then we went back to bed and slept well till dawn."

Kellan slid another foot down the fenceline, shaking his head. "Honestly, Ivy. What am I going to do with you?"

The expression on his face was a mixture of bewilderment, bemusement and frustration. I wanted to suggest he could take me on a date, but the timing was wrong. Besides, it really had to be his decision.

"For starters, you could tell me what kind of poison killed Edna," I said. "Do you know if she ate the crème brûlée in the evening or the morning?"

"Morning," he said. "It was strychnine, a medicine that nurses often carried to treat heart problems in the old days. Very toxic. Very fast. Very unpleasant."

The wheels in my head started turning. "She was killed by her own poison? When was it put in the crème brûlée? Can you tell?"

"We'll need advanced testing and that may never be clear." He slid another few inches. It was like he was being pulled away by a tractor beam, whereas Keats was just easing him gradually away from me. "Do you have any reason to believe Edna would take her own life?"

I shook my head. "I've thought about that a lot. She was obviously lonely and very unhappy, at least much of the time. But she took great pride in being a survivor. We talked about that as I drove her home the night before she died. I think she would have seen it as terribly weak to do that—especially when she'd gone to some lengths to arrange this event. Plus, she could have arranged an easier and more dignified passing if she'd wanted to go. Honestly, it seems more likely that one of the Bridge Buddies staged this."

"With what motivation? They seemed happier to have Edna alive to bully."

"They all had secrets. Edna must have known some of them." I shared the highlights of our discussion over dinner after Edna's death. "They were still resentful that she terrorized their kids, and you can't really blame them. We know that pain."

Kellan nodded. "But it's not enough to motivate a drastic move after all these years."

"They complained she was the gatekeeper at Doc Grainer's office. She might have collected some dirt on them there."

"Again, old news. But I'll look into it." He shifted another foot along the fence. "They're an odd group. When I told them that the death had been declared a murder, they barely looked up from their cards. And when I told them they'd have to stay here until I was ready to let them go home, they actually looked... happy."

"Of course they did," I said. "They get to indulge their addiction all day while Jilly and I wait on them hand and foot. I won't be able to charge them a penny extra since it isn't their choice to stay, either."

"Sorry," he said. "I hope you actually get to enjoy a group of guests some day. This one is as bad as the last."

I shook my head. "Nothing could be worse than the Flordale crew, because their presence brought back such miserable memories. With this group, the ringers are nice enough, but the Bridge Buddies try to keep us from talking to them, or even treating them like real guests. They're paid help."

"Interesting." His eyes glazed a little as he contemplated the puzzle before him. It was enough of a distraction that he didn't notice the canine puzzle beside him, easing him down the fence-line. Finally he said, "Now the real digging begins. Starting with Jilly's kitchen, I'm afraid."

"She cried when she saw the boxes, Kellan. Actual tears. You need to prioritize reuniting my friend with her stove."

"I'll move that to the top of my to-do list," he said, smirking. Then he looked around, suddenly alert. "Speaking of moving... what just happened?"

We were now at least six feet apart, and I burst out laughing at his expression. "You've been pranked," I said, gesturing to his feet.

Keats was panting ha-ha-ha while his tail lashed in satisfaction.

Kellan gave an exasperated sigh. "That dog just herded the Chief of Police without his knowledge or consent. He'd better not do that in front of my team. It's embarrassing."

"I'll stop him if he even entertains the thought," I said. "Are you feeling a little... sheepish?"

Kellan took a mock lunge at Keats and the dog ran off with a flourish of his tail.

"I heard you had a family meeting," he said. "How did that go?"

The smile left my face in a hurry. "They want me to give up the farm. Asher let it slip about Edna's passing not being an accident and Mom got everyone riled. She said the situation 'just isn't sustainable.'" I turned to watch the baby pygmy goats for a second.

There was no better way to switch emotional channels than with a trio of dancing kids. "It was hard hearing how upset they are about what's gone on here. But I don't back away from a challenge. Especially when animal welfare depends on it."

"I can certainly attest to that," he said. When I turned back from the goats, he gave me a smile that pretty much melted the soles off my work boots. "These animals are lucky to have you. Hannah chose her successor well."

I beamed at him, happier in that moment than I'd been in some time. If the baby goats frolicked or the alpaca danced I was completely unaware of it.

Finally Kellan broke the spell by saying, "Some day it would be nice to go out without the dog. A guy likes to call his own shots when it comes to things like that."

"Sounds great. I can speak to Keats about freeing up some time." I tried to sound cool when my heart was now frolicking like my giddy livestock. "On one condition."

"Oh?" He came closer again, apparently unaware of the black-and-white force pushing him in my direction. "What's that?"

"We'll need to take your vehicle. I refuse to go anywhere with you in Buttercup. She's a romance killer."

Kellan took a startled jump and turned. "Gah! He nipped me. If that mutt isn't a romance killer, I don't know what is."

"Enough, Keats." I was pretty sure the romance was still alive and breathing and I wanted to keep it that way. "I suppose if we can make it through a third murder together, we can survive a yellow jalopy and a jealous sheepdog."

Kellan laughed as he led me back to the house. "Amen to that."

CHAPTER TWELVE

"**R**elax," I told Keats, as we drove into town later. "It'll be fine."

He didn't answer or even look at me because he was too busy trying to keep his balance on the dashboard of the truck. I'd waited till all the cops were inside the farmhouse and then snuck off in my own truck like a devious teenager. I hadn't stalled once as I left, either, probably because I was still floating on a high from that smouldering smile Kellan gave me. I felt like I could do anything right now—even drive my own darn truck.

"Edna would be disgusted with me," I said. At that, Keats gave me a quick and curious glance. "A smile from a handsome man shouldn't make me so giddy... Not when there's a murder to solve. Specifically, hers."

The dog's ears came forward and he mumbled something that sounded like a question.

"Of course we're going to try to help," I said. "We owe it to Edna." After a successful left turn onto a side street I added, "Apparently I owe it to my family, too. And I most definitely owe it to myself to get the farm's reputation off the hook. Again."

I wasn't cocky enough to try parking the big beast on Main

Street in front of crowded noonday sidewalks, so I found a nice long spot nearby. From there, we walked to the Berry Good Café. It was my favorite little eatery in town, despite my having experienced several unsavory conversations on the back patio, including one with Kellan and another with a Flordale VP. I thought about trying to cleanse those memories with a short visit and a nice scone but decided to place my catering order and keep rolling. Jilly had her hands full with the cops desecrating her sanctuary.

I left Keats leashed to a lamppost outside—comfortable only because I could see him from the counter. Far from being stressed, his head swivelled this way and that, enjoying the view. All the world was a stage for this dog, and all the men and women merely players.

After arranging for meal delivery for the next couple of days, I left the café and ambled down Main Street with Keats by my side. When I first came home to Clover Grove, I'd felt like a stranger in a strange land. Many stores from my youth were long gone, replaced by cute new ones with fake antique facades and kitschy names. Two months later, the place had grown on me, although I wished everyone would stop trying so hard. It felt like a desperate bid to keep up with Dorset Hills, our more prosperous neighbor, which was impossible to recreate. Dog Town had lucked into a fabulous marketing angle at just the right time. Clover Grove should find its own, unique claim to fame.

As we passed Crowning Glory salon, Keats circled me and tightened the loop of the leash so fast he almost tripped me. "Hey. Rude," I said. "What's up with that?"

The door to the salon had opened with a jangle of bells just in time for Robbi Ford to hear me talking to my dog.

"What's up," she said with a chuckle, "is that you're in desperate need of a haircut, Ivy Galloway. Your cute pup obviously knows that, and you're in luck because I had a cancellation. The throne is empty."

"Oh, I couldn't, Roberta. Not today."

"Robbi," she reminded me. "I'll make it fast. You have no idea how good I am with scissors."

"Well..." I could certainly use a cut, and despite the fact that many, if not most, of Robbi's clients were seniors, I figured she could manage my mane just fine. Her own hair, long, lush and impeccably highlighted, was the perfect advertisement for her services.

"I'll sweeten the deal with a latte," she said. "I have a high-end machine in here."

"Done." I spun to unfurl the leash from my legs and let Keats pull me inside.

Robbi headed to a coffee station in the back corner of the small salon. Crowning Glory managed to pull off cute without being completely overdone. There were two chairs covered in red vinyl with gold trim that actually did look like thrones, only more comfortable, and the big oval mirrors in front of the chairs were surrounded by ornate filigree. When Robbi came back, a pretty floral teacup rattled gently on its saucer. Two sugar cubes sat beside the cup with tiny silver tongs. She waited for me to add one of the cubes and then offered me a sterling teaspoon.

"Wow," I said, taking the cup and teaspoon. "I feel better already. You treat people like royalty. No wonder you're so popular with the bridge club."

She laughed again, and I knew that melodious sound was part of her charm. No matter what tales she heard as she snipped, she probably ended every session with a reassuring laugh that made the town's leading ladies feel like queens.

"I'm pretty good with my magic wand, too," she said, picking up a pair of scissors from a little cart and waving them.

"Just a quick trim, please. Things are a bit crazy at the inn today."

Keats herded me none too subtly toward the chair with nudges and outright pokes with his long nose. Since when did he care about how my hair looked? Did he even understand what went on here? I sighed and sat down. Maybe he wanted me to look good for my future date with Kellan. When push came to nudge with Keats, I usually took his lead.

"I heard about Edna," Robbi said, and her smile slipped away. "She was a valued client for many years. We'd even become friends, of a sort, which few could likely say. She was very private."

Ah, so *that's* why Keats wanted me to come in. Perhaps Robbi had intel on the Bridge Buddies, and which one of them was most likely to poison. And here I thought he'd become a romantic. Well, in the interests of sleuthing, I was willing to part with my locks.

Robbi released the messy bun I'd twisted and clipped before Aladdin crowed at dawn. Sometimes my scalp hurt from leaving my hair up too long, but leaving it loose was an occupational hazard.

"My appearance is the last thing I worry about these days," I admitted. "But I'd probably feel better if I looked better."

Robbi's smile came back. "Exactly my philosophy. And Edna's too, believe it or not. That's why she decided last minute to get a perm the day before the event at your inn. She didn't want a hair out of place." She gave a heavy sigh. "Now it will stay perfect forever."

Keats sat just far enough away to avoid getting stepped on but close enough to hear every word. Meanwhile, Robbi wasted no time in starting to dry cut. The first cut was definitely the deepest and she gave me a reassuring smile in the mirror when I gasped. I suppose she knew a bold move was the only way to get me to part with any of it. Once that cut was made, there was no turning back, so I decided to surrender to the process.

"Edna's perm caused a tempest in a teapot," I said, when it seemed safe to distract her. "The Bridge Buddies were up in arms because it spilled into Annamae's standing appointment."

Robbi gave a cluck of disapproval. "I value my longstanding clients, Ivy, really I do, but sometimes it's like negotiating between warring nations. Annamae didn't seem that upset, but the others... *oh my.* I even offered to do a home visit for Annamae the same day. It's nice to get out of here sometimes, although I lose more scissors that way." She laughed as she snipped away half a year of growth. "Once people realize how sharp professional shears are, they never want to return them."

"I bet people prefer to come here for the experience," I said. "It's nice to take a break in your throne."

"That's how most people feel," she said, her smile returning. "The seniors especially look forward to getting out and catching up."

"Mom says your salon is a social hub for the community. It's where everything happens with the town matrons."

Again, Robbi's smile wavered and failed. "I am so sorry about what happened with your mom. Dahlia was bullied out of here, no two ways about it. They tried it with Edna, too."

"Mom's doing fine," I said. "She made Iris learn hairstyling basics online and every time I see her, it looks more polished and professional."

Robbi nodded. "One day, she can come back. This won't go on forever."

She seemed to be implying that the ruling hair class would eventually graduate to the great beyond, leaving some available slots for people like Mom, who wasn't one of the cool girls.

"You're the only game in town," I said. "It's like a turf war."

"And yet my business is far from booming." She gestured to the empty throne. "I can't seem to pull in a younger crowd, and believe me, I'd love to." She gave my hair a toss and a dramatic snip. "This is far more fun than repeating the same set every week for my seniors. You're going to be a walking billboard."

I laughed. "You could do better. I'll send Jilly one day."

"You do that. I'd banked on Clover Grove catching up to Dog Town a little faster, but we're the turtles."

Glancing down, I saw Keats giving me a piercing stare. I got the point. Less chitchat, more sleuthing.

"I admired Edna's resilience," I said, watching Robbi in the mirror. "The bridge club was hard on her that last day."

"Make that every day," Robbi said. "They didn't like the secrets she knew. As the town's only nurse for decades, she had access to all the juicy stories. Old news now, of course, and far beyond the current club."

I grinned up at her. "How juicy?"

"Affairs, pregnancies, STDS, you name it. Someone had an abortion without her husband knowing. Another husband got a vasectomy without his wife knowing, which broke her heart when she found out, since she wanted more kids." She sighed as she snipped. "That's not even touching on the real ailments."

"Edna told you all this?" I concealed my shock with the poker face I'd perfected over a decade in HR.

Robbi shook her head quickly. "Clients shared their own stories, and most of them have passed, now. But everyone knew Edna was aware of these things and they resented it. Edna was always discreet, however, at least with me."

My mind was spinning a bit from all this information but Keats stared at me intently, as if warning me to keep a cool head.

"Maybe one of my current guests wanted Edna gone," I said.

Robbi shrugged and met my eyes in the ornate mirror. "Even if they had secrets worth hiding, they'd be decades old. I don't see why Gertrude, Morag or Joan would snap like that now. Sweet Annamae simply isn't capable."

I knew from experience that seemingly sweet people could do terrible things, but I tended to agree that old stories like these would have been filed away by now. "I guess these women have tortured themselves and each other with secret-keeping for decades. No wonder it feels like a powder keg. When they're not playing bridge, that is. Once the cards are in hand, the air clears."

"Interesting," Robbi said, spinning the throne to cut a long fringe around my face. "Even the small things caused tension. Who tipped the best, who brought in the best cookies, who dared to try a new cut or color. It was like dancing naked in a minefield."

I laughed at the image. "You deserve danger pay, Robbi."

Standing back, she appraised me and gave a few last, dramatic snips. "And yet I love my job, and love my clients. I just want everyone to get along and I do my best to keep the peace. I'm only telling you this now because I want justice for Edna."

I nodded but her left hand clamped down on my head. "Don't move. I'm about to finish a work of art."

"Kellan Harper will want to talk to you," I said.

"I look forward to it," she said, grinning. "Maybe he'll even thank me for the good work I did today."

"For sharing Bridge Buddy politics?" I asked.

Stepping back, she twirled the chair so that I faced the ornate mirror. "For turning his beauty into a princess. Now... let's get you washed and blown out."

KEATS PULLED me out of the shop even harder than he'd pulled me in. It was as if he couldn't shake the dark clumps of my hair off his snowy paws fast enough. He shook himself thoroughly and repeatedly, and his tail and ears drooped. I felt similarly grimy, but on the inside, from hearing the salacious tales of the Clover Grove elite. Why I thought it would be different here than anywhere else, I didn't know. After what I used to hear about the private lives of Flordale staff, I thought nothing would shock me. It turned out I wasn't immune after all.

Nearly a block away, an older woman with frizzy gray curls

and an oversized coat that flapped in the breeze stepped in front of me. "You're the youngest Galloway girl, right? The one with the farm?"

"That's right. I'm Ivy and this is Keats."

His tail came up and the white tuft waved. Either he liked her or he just liked being out and about again.

"I'm Maud Burnett. I went to school with your grandmother, Gardenia." She paused for a moment. "Oh, how she hated that name."

I laughed. "Floral names are the family curse. I figure I got lucky at the end of the line."

"Well, you're a lovely girl with a lovely name," Maud said. "I was hoping you'd do something lovely now in memory of Edna Evans."

"I'll do my best," I said. "Were you and Edna friends?"

"I tried," Maud said. "Edna didn't find friendship easy. But I'm very sorry she passed, and in the way she did. It wasn't right."

"No, it wasn't," I said. "I'm sure the police will figure out what happened."

"I hope so, but they'll have to cast a wide net. Edna had some detractors, as I'm sure you know. I hope your handsome brother will talk to Ted Tupper. He's the one who petitioned to get Edna fired as school nurse. They retired her early, and it was a hit to her pride and her pension."

"I'll mention that to the police," I said.

"Mention Linda Snead as well. Edna blamed a bout of salmonella on crab salad from Linda's deli and ultimately the business shuttered due to the gossip. You know what this town is like."

I nodded. "I sure do. Is that all?"

"Well, they're already looking into the bridge club, I'm sure. But it might not be a bad idea to talk to Helen Randall over in Dorset Hills. She's had nothing but harsh words for Edna for decades now."

"And how did Edna harm Helen?" I asked. It was almost comical how many enemies Edna had amassed over a lifetime.

"She broke her husband's heart, that's how."

My eyes widened. "Pardon me?"

"Before they were married, of course. It sounds like Merle Randall never got over Edna and poor Helen felt like the second-hand rose."

"Ah, right. Merle, her former fiancé."

Maud nodded. "I'm surprised she mentioned him at all. She must have liked you."

"I think we were forging a bond," I said. "As you say, she found that difficult."

Maud clutched my arm. "What I really wanted to ask was whether you'd look after Edna's cats. You being an animal lover and all, I figured you wouldn't let them starve. There are so many of them and they probably can't fend for themselves anymore."

"Cats? I was over there every day, Maud, and never saw a single cat."

"It's a feral colony, and I only know about it because I still work part-time at the post office. She got a huge shipment of cat food and veterinary supplies delivered just last week, so they're still around."

I glanced at Keats and found him watching Maud with his head tipped and his ears forward. He was interested in this line of discussion. Very interested, indeed.

"Maud, I promise to look into everything you've said. If you think of anything else, don't hesitate to call me at Runaway Farm."

"I won't, Ivy. And if you'd like me to say a few words at the funeral, I'd be honored. I assume you're taking care of the arrangements."

Add something else to my ever-growing to-do list.

CHAPTER THIRTEEN

"What do you say about a walk, buddy?" I asked, on the drive home. "Maybe we should look for those feral cats before they get too hungry."

Keats mumbled enthusiastic agreement. I knew this was an errand he'd embrace with glee. One of his few shortcomings in my eyes was being a cat-hater. The two barn cats who lived at the farm when we arrived had shipped out soon after.

"Look, if we find them, you've got to be nice. I'm really not thrilled that you rousted our barn cats, you know. You'd better take up mousing if you intend to fill all roles."

He treated me with a cool blue-eyed stare that said, "Never going to happen." It's not like he wasn't capable, but he had bigger priorities. That left Charlie dealing with the increasing rodent population in ways I didn't want to know about. Hannah had owned a terrier, Prima, who was a dedicated hunter, but we were losing the battle she'd won.

As we pulled up at Edna's house I complimented myself on another drive without a single stall. I was on a roll. Kellan should flirt with me more often—and maybe he would now that I had a rather stunning new hairdo. I tipped the rearview mirror and admired the gleaming, stylish cut. Honestly, my hair had never looked so good. Back in Boston, I'd kept it in a take-me-seriously bob. Now there were flowing layers that started at my chin, which meant I could still sweep it up and away. But when I wanted to look date-worthy, I had options. Robbi really knew her stuff.

Keats mumbled something akin to, "Stop ogling yourself," and I laughed. He wasn't used to my spending a single second on vanity.

"Get used to it, buddy. Kellan is a handsome man. He deserves a little effort."

If a dog could grunt in disgust, that was the sound he made now. Then he panted ha-ha-ha to get me moving. He was all over this feral colony idea.

"Don't get your hopes up," I said, getting out of the truck. "Maud may be wrong. In fact, Edna mentioned her disgust for all things feline more than once and I'm hard pressed to imagine she'd cater to an entire colony. But if there are hungry cats missing her, I need to check."

The first thing we did was check the two large back sheds, which thankfully, weren't even locked. There was nothing inside to give me pause. Or paws. I smiled at my own silent joke and Keats practically rolled his eyes.

"Is there anyplace else to search?" I asked. "Use your nose."

He did just that, lowering it like a bloodhound. After a couple of wide circles, he headed into the bush on the far side of Edna's property, away from the farm. I never came over this way as the land was spotted with small marshes.

Before long, Keats gave a sharp bark of triumph. There was a trim, grey, relatively new metal shed squatting in thick brush. This one was also unlocked, so I turned on my phone light and stepped inside.

Sure enough, there were half a dozen large bags of cat kibble and dozens of gallon jugs of water. On a higher shelf were boxes of flea treatments and an arsenal of other supplies feral cats might need to stay healthy.

In one corner sat a wheelbarrow, which I assumed Edna used to transport the goods to the cats. It couldn't be that far. As fit as Edna was for 80, wheeling food and water around rough trails must have been challenging.

"That's one way to stay fit," I said, filling the wheelbarrow now. "I'm going to need you to play hound again, okay?"

His tail swished and soon he was leading me into the bush with his nose to the ground.

"Slow down," I called. "This thing is tippy."

It was probably only 20 minutes but it felt like forever to my aching arms when I hit the last knobby root, righted the wheelbarrow, and looked up to see a wide open space.

"Huckleberry Marsh!" I recognized it instantly from my childhood. My brother had brought me down here a few times, decades ago. He and his friends spent many a day here and even a few nights in the clubhouse they built. I could see it now, across a good-sized pond. The rough-hewn building looked the worse for years of neglect, but the white skull and crossbones Asher had painted still showed faintly. The words "Keep Out" had faded away, but I was more than happy to do so. I never felt comfortable here, even with my brother.

Many of the old trees had died, waterlogged by the expanding, murky pond. Thick green moss covered many of them and ivy dripped off their naked boughs. The pond itself still featured the unique criss-crossed logs the boys used to create a highway across the shallow portions of the marsh. My brother and his friends would be thrilled to hear the network had stood the test of time. I doubted anyone had been here for years, or Edna wouldn't have chosen the site to host her feline friends.

I noticed the first cat, a large shiny black one resembling a panther, flitting across the log highway. Keats gave a loud wuff and charged.

That didn't go well. He promptly slid off the log and ended up with his white feet in gloppy green swamp silt. Keats was not a fan of either water or muddy feet and he immediately slunk back to sit beside me.

"I told you to be nice," I said. "Now look what happened."

Suddenly cats were popping up everywhere, from behind trees and out from under logs. There were coats in every color and pattern imaginable. A large, fluffy, dark marmalade cat appeared on top of the stone wall of the fortress my brother and his buddies built one summer. Big Red had a confident look about him, as if he ran the place. Then the black panther jumped up beside him and a white cat joined them. She was delicate where the others were brawny but her coat was pristine. I couldn't help but think about Annamae's accusation that Edna had stolen her cat, Fleecy. I had the distinct impression that these cats were quite happy here, and they certainly looked healthy. No matter how they arrived, Edna had clearly been caring for them well.

"What can I use to hold water?" I said. "I'm not going into that shack. It was creepy way back when and it's even creepier now. Who knows what those boys left in there? It's probably booby-trapped."

Keats lifted a muddy paw, shook it gingerly and then offered a point toward the stone wall. "Is that the feeding station?" I asked. "Okay. Makes sense." I picked up a bag of food, hoisted it over my shoulder and said, "Kitties, I'm coming. Don't be scared. I like cats, even if Keats doesn't. We don't agree on everything."

The real challenge was crossing a long mossy log to get there while wearing clunky work boots and balancing an awkwardly heavy bag. I was far from elegant at the best of times. Yet Edna must have managed a similar feat.

More cats gathered on the wall as if to watch the show. I recognized an exceptionally gorgeous gray tabby with a bullseye on his side.

"Hey, I know you," I called as I picked my way over the log carefully. "You'd rather live in swampland than a nice warm barn? Winter's coming, you know. You can still come home. Bring a couple of friends." I took a few more steps. "Mind you, I'd expect y'all to work for your wages. Obviously Edna gives you a free ride."

I heaved a sigh of relief when I reached the other side and tossed the bag of food onto the ground. The air was dank and heavy with the smell of moss and rotting wood, but it wasn't as noxious as Wilma's pig pool. The thought made me shudder, and I looked up at the cats. "I'm sorry to tell you that Edna won't be coming around anymore. Something terrible happened, but maybe you already know that." The black cat jumped down, came over and stared up at me with big green eyes. "I'm going to take care of you now," I said. He let out a sound that was half purr, half meow. "You're welcome. It's an honor, really."

Some of the other cats fled as I walked to the stone wall and peered over, but Big Red and Fleecy held their ground. On the other side of the barricade was a makeshift shelter made of cheap plywood that sheltered nearly two dozen large stainless steel mixing bowls. At least half of them were already filled, and there were several jugs of fresh water.

"She left you well supplied," I said. "No one's gone hungry here."

I walked around the fortress, collected the empty bowls and walked back. With difficulty, I tore open the big bag of food and poured kibble into bowl after bowl. Then I replaced them and carried the jugs of water around. Since they weren't all needed, I lined them up against the wall.

"I assume you're sharing your bounty with the local wildlife," I said. "So I thank you for keeping them away from my livestock."

I looked up when I heard a keening wail. Keats was sitting at the other end of the log bridge, wanting to come over but too scared. This dog didn't hesitate to attack a murderous human but he was afraid of swamp water.

"I'll be right back, buddy. Almost done here."

I'd assumed that the cats would be too wild to let me touch them, but the panther and Fleecy rubbed up against me from the top of the wall. Big Red held back, blinking with yellowy eyes. I got the same odd feeling as when Keats gave me a stare with his blue eye. It was as if Red could see into my soul.

"I hope you like what you see, Red, because I'll be back." I shook my head. "As if I don't have my hands full already. But winter's coming and it'll be easier to get around out here when it freezes."

Keats gave another whine, louder this time. Rolling up the empty food bag, I tucked it into my overalls and turned to go. It would be nice to have my arms free to balance on the way back.

I was about halfway across when Keats finally summoned the nerve to join me. "No, Keats, go back. I'm almost there."

He continued toward me, growling.

I don't know how Big Red got around me, but he pulled off the athletic feat and charged at Keats. There was a collision of sound—barking, hissing and an unearthly yowl that might have come from either one of them. A dozen or so other cats circled me, too, and my arms pinwheeled.

It was no use. I slid off the log at the same time as Keats, and we landed with twin splashes. The water wasn't deep but the bottom was so silty that I floundered and thrashed as I tried to gain purchase, and then went under briefly.

Surfacing, I let out a yowl not dissimilar to the one the critters had unleashed moments before. "My hair!"

Thrashing through the water, I got out on the far side of the pond, where Keats was already shaking himself and coughing dramatically.

"This is all your fault," I said, stomping ahead of him to the trail. "You had to go and growl at them, didn't you? I can never have nice things."

I fumed all the way back, pushing the empty wheelbarrow. Long before we reached Edna's yard, however, Keats' tail was high and waving. The dirt seemed to be drying and falling away from his white plume, and even his paws.

The same couldn't be said for my hair "don't." Twisting it up, I secured it with the tie from my sodden front pocket. "I'll have some explaining to do to my guests, I'm afraid."

I stalled the truck once on Edna's lane, but that was only because three cats that looked very much like Panther, Fleecy and Big Red—the senior cat counsel—ran across the road.

"Whatever," I yelled. I'd rolled all the windows down to release the mossy stink. "Have the last laugh, ingrates!"

Keats mumbled something that was quite likely canine profanity. Then he went back to licking his paws and ignored me completely.

CHAPTER FOURTEEN

It was nice to be able to call Kellan with some leads I'd gained without sacrificing anything more than a few inches of hair. He didn't seem to find it strange that I'd pamper myself in a salon at a busy and stressful time. Perhaps he thought even down-to-earth women like me worked in mysterious ways.

Since the discussion went so well, I didn't bother to mention that it was Keats' idea to go into Crowning Glory. The dog got plenty of credit and was getting a bit cocky as it was. I was almost glad he got a dunk in the swamp to remind him he was fallible.

Kellan decided to come back to the farm that afternoon to interview the Bridge Buddies all over again and see if he could stir up some old grudges, without implicating Robbi or having access to medical files to prove anything. I really wanted to have those conversations myself, but Kellan was trained at interrogation and far preferred it when I kept my nose out of it.

His presence at the inn meant Jilly and I could drive into town to pick up a few things. We were already standing beside Buttercup when he pulled up in the police SUV.

"Wow," he said, as he got out. "Did you do something to your hair?"

"Yeah." I felt a flush start in my midriff and head north as Jilly turned to offer a sly smirk. "It's been through some trauma lately."

"Looks nice to me," he said, smiling. "Traumatized hair suits you."

Jilly continued to smirk and I continued to blush as Kellan made his way up to the house. The second the door closed behind him, I gestured to the truck and we abandoned Buttercup. Both of us giggled like guilty teens as we bunny-hopped down the lane. Even Keats preferred the belligerent pickup, as it gave him a higher vantage point to monitor the world.

Our first stop in town was the Berry Good Café, where Jilly revised my catering order. Apparently my taste was about as upscale as my overalls and she still cared to give our guests a positive culinary experience. The Bridge Buddies barely seemed to notice what they were eating and probably would have been just as happy with a meal replacement drink so they could play on.

When Jilly was finished with her errands, I suggested a stroll through town. It was a fresh, sunny day and the break did us a world of good... especially because I didn't trouble her by mentioning that we had a couple more stops.

"Do you want to grab an ice cream?" I asked, stopping outside Triple Threat, a café, grocery store and ice cream parlor all in one.

"Not really. It's a little cool for ice cream, isn't it?"

"It's never too cool for ice cream," I said. "It might be our last chance at a triple cone till spring."

"I ordered a chocolate mousse cake for dinner. I'll hold out for that."

"Suit yourself," I said, looping Keats' leash around the railing. "I'm going in."

Ted Tupper, the bald and brawny proprietor, served me himself. I would rather have done the questioning before I had the triple cone in my hand, but sometimes a sleuth has to roll with the scoops. And they were very generous scoops. It was like he wanted to use up the ice cream for the season.

"That's a mix I haven't seen before," Ted said, packing another half-scoop on the already massive pile. "You might regret that later."

I regretted it already, because it started to drip the second he handed it to me. It might have been cool outside but apparently Ted liked to keep it tropical inside to keep selling cones.

It was all I could do to get the cash out of my front pocket before ice cream coated the back of my hand.

Glancing out the window, I raised the cone at Jilly and grinned. She just rolled her eyes and said something to Keats, likely unflattering.

Making a show of looking at his name tag, I said, "Ted, I'm Ivy Galloway, and I run an inn at Runaway Farm. I might be looking at a bit of catering this week."

"Hey, Ivy. I heard your kitchen is down after what happened to Edna Evans. Can't say I'm sorry to see the last of her, though. She came in every week for a child-sized vanilla cone. I think she just enjoyed riling me."

I tried to lick the cone while mopping up my hand with napkins at the same time. "You two have a falling-out?"

He gave me a strange look. "I guess you didn't keep up on local news when you were away."

"I wanted to put some distance between Clover Grove and me back then," I said. "I've only been home a couple of months so I'm still way behind."

"Well, I had Edna Evans fired," he said. Beckoning, he came around the end of the counter and led me to the small seating area. "Let me tell you the story."

I was grateful for the opportunity to sit down and let the table catch the drips rather than the front of my overalls. "You mean as school nurse?" I asked. "She was pretty brutal with those vaccinations."

"Sadistic, more like. The faster you ran, the harder she got you." He shook his head. "Man, she could move in those days."

"My brother said the same thing. Once he hid under a stage for eight hours but eventually she dragged him down the hall by his feet. She was like a pro wrestler."

Ted grabbed some napkins from my pile and patted his forehead, which was beading with sweat at the memory.

He looked up as Jilly joined us and I introduced her quickly. "Ted's just telling me about his experiences with Edna as school nurse."

"Ah," she said. "Carry on. But slide over so I can keep my eye on Keats."

I gave her a grateful smile and tried to hand her the cone, which she declined. Friendship only went so far.

"I had this recurring nightmare about Edna chasing me through the school's back field," Ted said, taking more of the napkins I needed. "That actually happened, so I guess it was PTSD. Finally I decided to do something about it and see if I could end the dreams."

"And what did you do?" I chased dribbles up my wrist with my tongue, since my napkins were gone. Shaking her head, Jilly got up to collect a fresh pile from the counter.

"First I contacted the school board but they wouldn't take action, even though she was still traumatizing kids, twenty years later. Then I tried Doc Grainer, and he didn't want to hear it, either. So finally I started a petition. Hundreds and hundreds of people signed it, including your brother and all your sisters. Thanks to the Internet, the whole thing snowballed and hit the media, and then the school board had no choice but to sit up and take notice."

I wrapped a thick wad of napkins around the cone. "That's when they fired her?"

"I wish. Instead they retired her early on a reduced pension. Doc Grainer never let her go, but at least I'd done *something*."

"I'm sure she took it pretty hard," I said, barely staying ahead of the melting confection.

"Not hard enough." It seemed like his entire bald head creased in a frown. "She seemed to be living the good life, with her nice little house and her bridge games, showing up here for her kiddie cone. Meanwhile the rest of us suffered."

"The nightmares didn't stop?" I asked.

"Trailed off over the years, and maybe they'll end now as I think about her in that swamp." He stared at me with hungry eyes. "You saw her, right?"

"I did, Ted. And as much as you have nightmares, I'll have some about that." I gave up and set the cone down on the remaining napkins. "Trust me, you don't want that image running through your mind."

"Don't be so sure about that." Raising his hand, he called, "Linda, can you join us?"

A short, plump redhead came out from behind the counter. "What's going on, Ted?"

Ted introduced Jilly and me. "Honey, Ivy wants to hear about what happened with Edna. Ladies, my wife Linda is the happy ending to my story."

Linda took the seat beside him. "It wasn't the happiest beginning, but it has worked out rather nicely for us both."

"Edna basically forced Linda's deli out of business by spreading malicious gossip about food poisoning," Ted said.

"The county's public health rep had the crab salad tested—and everything else in the place—and there was no salmonella," Linda said. "But by then the rumor mill was working overtime. There was no convincing people my deli was safe, and business shut off like a faucet. I had no choice but to close. You can't make a living in this town with a bad reputation, even if it's false."

I glanced at Jilly and we both nodded. "I have reason to worry about that myself," I said. "That's why I'm so curious about what happened to Edna."

"Someone finally caught up with her," Linda said, with a huge smile that seemed to show every tooth. "I can't say I'm sorry it was poison. I think they call that divine justice."

"Good riddance to bad garbage," Ted said. He gathered the big pile of napkins along with my cone and got up to dump them in the trash. "But out of the worst compost, beautiful things may grow."

Linda's smile resized to normal. "Ted has such a way with words. I came to him for advice on dealing with Edna's slander, and while it was too late for my deli, the timing was just right for us. Now we run Triple Threat together and couldn't be happier."

"What a unique how-we-met story," Jilly said, beaming at them like the true romantic she was. "Something to tell your grandkids one day."

"That's right," Ted said, touching his wife's shoulder gently. "I'm grateful for how things worked out in the end. But I'm also grateful someone ended Edna. I wish I could offer them free cones for life."

"Oh, Ted," Linda said. "A murder in our community is never good news, and it's causing trouble for Ivy."

"I'm sure the inn will be fine," Jilly said, getting up from the table. "As you say, Linda, sometimes you have to trust in divine justice."

"Would you like to meet my dog?" I asked. "Keats loves people and I'd hate to disappoint him."

Jilly raised skeptical eyebrows and I grinned at her as we followed the happy couple outside. Keats was far from a people pleaser, but he obliged now with an enthusiastic wag, probably only because he'd been left alone for longer than he'd like.

"What was that about?" Jilly asked, as we walked back to the truck.

"Just getting Keats' take on Ted and Linda. They were a little too gleeful about Edna's death for my liking. But they got a pass from Keats."

"Well, maybe divine justice *will* take care of things for the inn, too," she said.

"I wish I could count on that, but I'm guessing there's one heck of a line up ahead of us," I said. "Even in Clover Grove."

"WHERE ARE WE?" Jilly asked, as I pulled up outside a large, pretty house on the outskirts of town. The landscaping was impeccable, with the last of the hardy flowers putting up a brave front beside red Japanese maples.

"We're just dropping by to say hello to Kathleen Mayfair," I said. "People still do that out here. Drop by and say hello."

Jilly was instantly suspicious. "Maybe my question should be, *why* are we? Here, that is. I've never heard you mention a Kathleen Mayfair."

"Her maiden name was Grainer."

My friend gave an exasperated sigh. "As in Old Doc Grainer. Edna's former boss."

"Precisely. You have a great memory for details, my friend." Opening the door, I released Keats. "I just want to make sure she's heard about Edna."

"Please. She heard about Edna almost before it happened. I already know this town's ability to spread gossip at lightening speed all too well." She opened the passenger door. "What are we *really* here for? You can't think Doc Grainer's daughter had anything to do with Edna's death."

Coming around the truck to join her, I shook my head. "Honestly, it is a drop-in. After all the negativity, I guess I just want to hear another point of view."

Kathleen opened the door at the first knock and I was surprised to see how much she'd aged. She was my mom's age, but obviously there was something to be said for rotational dating. Mom fought aging with the ferocity of a cougar, and she was coming out on top.

"Ivy," she said, stepping back to let us in. "How lovely to see you and your beautiful friend. Not to mention a very handsome dog." Keats offered a brisk swish of his white plume, giving Kathleen a gold star in the character department. "Can I make you a coffee?"

"We'd love a coffee," I said. "I hope you don't mind a drop-in."

"Not at all. You know how we old-timers are: there's always a cake in the house, just in case."

Mom didn't operate that way, but it was a quaint tradition and normally I'd be all over it. The triple cone had taken the edge off my appetite, but as we chatted I worked my way valiantly through the generous wedge of coconut cake she set before me, and Jilly did the same.

"I suppose you heard about Edna," I said, after a respectable interval.

Kathleen nodded. "I'd like to say a few words at the funeral, if you're making arrangements."

"I certainly intend to help out." If Edna had a will or an executor, Kellan hadn't mentioned it yet. "Were you fond of her?"

"Well, fond would be the wrong word," Kathleen said, tactfully. "She didn't exactly promote fondness. I respected her, though... because my father did."

"They worked together for decades, as I recall."

"He said he couldn't do his job without her—that when Edna said jump, he asked how high." Sipping her coffee thoughtfully, she added, "Dad also said she helped him diagnose many a difficult case. That in another era, she'd have made a brilliant doctor. His words, not mine."

"Wow, that's very high praise," I said, forcing down another mouthful of cake. "She told me it wasn't easy having a career in her day."

"Three choices, right?" Jilly said. "Nurse, teacher or secretary."

"Exactly," Kathleen said. "I chose teacher, which is how I know that Edna was also tough on children. There was something a little dark there."

"True. I was the recipient of many of her gleeful vaccinations." I set my fork down, unable to take one more bite. "Maybe it's because her hopes for a family blew up."

"She told you?" Kathleen said, clearly surprised.

"The day before she passed, actually. I was sorry to hear about her heartbreak."

"There was a terrible misunderstanding and they were both too proud to heal the rift. Merle Randall was a lovely man. *Is* a lovely man," she corrected herself. "Still very much alive in Dorset Hills."

I downed most of my coffee in one gulp before saying, "Maybe regrets about pride are exactly why she told me about it. I let pride stand in the way of healing a rift for a long time."

Kathleen grinned at me over the rim of her cup. "I ran into your mother. She's practically planning your wedding to Chief Harper already."

Looking helplessly at Jilly, I saw a similar grin above her cup. "Me, too," she said. "It'll be the event of the season."

"Let us have a date first," I said, getting up.

"You had plenty back in school," Kathleen said. "I saw you two mooning over each other. Seize the day, young lady. As a doctor's daughter, I feel qualified to remind you that you never know how long you've got."

"Heard and understood." I let Keats lead us to the front door.

"Do you have any idea who might have wished Edna ill? I mean, beyond every child who suffered her needles?"

"I've given that a lot of thought," Kathleen said, as she opened the front door. "The only people I knew to speak ill of Edna openly were members of her bridge club. Personally, I think they were worried she'd spill secrets that came out in my father's office. But Edna valued her job too much to do that. Perhaps something blew up on that front eventually."

"Were they the type of secrets that could blow up decades later?" I asked.

"Perhaps." Kathleen winked at me. "Secrets have a nasty way of doing that, don't they?"

Before I could press further, she closed the door on the discussion with a firm click.

"You're dying to talk to Merle, aren't you?" Jilly asked, as we climbed into the truck.

"And his wife," I said. "But how about I leave that to Kellan, just to make you happy?"

"Don't make promises you can't keep, my friend," she said.

"Then I won't promise to eat any of that chocolate mousse cake you ordered," I said. "Because a bumpy ride home is going to do some terrible things to my innards."

"That's the price a wannabe sleuth has to pay," she said.

"I know you enjoy a little investigation, too, Jilly, no matter what you say."

She gave an uncharacteristic snort. "What gave you that idea?"

"Because you just welcomed Keats into your lap without his even asking. You've got a detective buzz."

"I've got a sugar buzz," she said, as his tail dusted her face.

After we drove for a while, I said, "It's hard to reconcile the many sides of Edna, isn't it? She was loathed by children, yet saved lives with Old Doc Grainer. She fed feral cats, yet she was a mean and nosy neighbor."

"It's a good thing we had cutthroat corporate careers before moving here," Jilly said. "Otherwise we probably wouldn't survive the complexities of the simple life."

"Good point," I said. "I used to hate being known as the grim reaper. Now I see it as a distinct advantage because you can't keep a grim reaper down." Rolling down the window, I let the air blow through my hair. "Remind me to pick up a scythe."

CHAPTER FIFTEEN

We didn't make it back to the farm before my phone buzzed with a summons: "Mafia 911. Chow Chow. ASAP."

"Are we in the Rescue Mafia now?" Jilly asked, staring at my phone while I made a rather treacherous U-turn and headed in the opposite direction.

I geared up surprisingly smoothly. It was as if the truck enjoyed a special mission as much as the rest of us. "At best we're in the minors. From what Charlie says, there's a lot of auditioning and hazing from Cori Hogan before you hit the major league. We haven't done any hard-core rescues yet. Archie the calf and a handful of hens wouldn't count."

"But we've contributed to murder investigations. And you've confronted stone-cold killers."

I shook my head. "Those were just humans. To make the grade with the Rescue Mafia, it's all about animals, and more specifically dogs."

"Keats doesn't count?" She tried to adjust him on her lap. When she'd invited him aboard, she hadn't expected such a long ride. "That was a pretty spectacular rescue."

"True. And it counted with Hannah, since it got me the farm.

Cori's a little harder to impress. She's all about climbing and ziplining and elaborate schemes. The black ops of the rescue world."

Jilly laughed. "I'll stick to the minors, thank you very much. I've had enough adventure in the past few months to last me a while."

Keats braced himself on the dash, ears forward, tail up. He was leaning right into whatever adventure awaited. An adrenaline junkie.

My attitude was somewhere in the middle. A little adventure now and then was good to make you appreciate the peace of regular life. But a long string of murder investigations I did not need.

We passed the first of many huge bronze Labrador Retriever statues that marked the perimeter of Dorset Hills and turned right to circle the city. The chow chow meet spot was on the far side of Dog Town. We both fell silent, and I started speculating. Last time it had been a small group. With it being an emergency, we could be even more outnumbered. Yes, I'd faced stone-cold killers but it was never voluntary. Somehow these women were equally daunting—a force of nature.

Bridget's battered old lime-green van sat in the parking lot at the base of the trail beside Remi's sedan and an SUV. It was early afternoon now and the sun was still high enough to light the trail. It helped that much of the foliage had fallen away. Still, it was heavy going and I wondered why City Council had seen fit to place one of the more stunning statues way out here where few ever saw it.

"It's about time," Cori said, as we trudged into the clearing. In addition to Bridget and Remi and Andrea, there was another redhead and a beautiful blonde woman I recognized as Arianna Torrance, a dog breeder.

"We couldn't have arrived faster without teleporting," I said, shaking my head as Keats frolicked around her like a starstruck teenager. "We were already in the truck outside of Clover Grove."

Cori raised her orange-fingered glove and looked at Remi. "Tell her I don't like excuses."

"I'm quite sure she heard you," Remi said, laughing. "And probably knew it already. It kind of goes with the gloves."

Flexing her fingers, Cori tipped her head like a little brown bird. "We only 911 if it's something critical. Obviously."

A woman with a head of curly red hair and bright green eyes stepped forward and offered her hand to me and then Jilly. "We haven't met. I'm Evie Springdale."

"We loved your show!" Jilly's voice overlapped with mine.

Evie was the creator and producer of The Princess and the Pig, which chronicled Hannah's early days at Runaway Farm.

"I watched it over and over, trying to learn every nuance about the farm," I said. "Thank you for that. You're a cat lover, right?"

"I do love my Roberto," she said, smiling. "Having married a veterinarian, however, I'm expanding my horizons as far and as fast as my allergy meds allow."

I told them about Edna's feral cat colony. "I saw at least twenty cats, and those were just the bold ones."

"The cat colony is kind of redeeming, right?" Evie said, turning to her friends.

"Definitely," Remi said. "So Edna wasn't all bad."

Cori threw them a glare. "Well she certainly wasn't good. You've heard the stories."

"We were just talking about that in the truck," Jilly said. "There's so much gray area in life, isn't there?"

"Saving a few cats doesn't cancel out all the negatives," Cori said. "And this Edna had plenty of blots on her character."

"But it's a mitigating factor," I said.

Cori shrugged. "She's got a lot to mitigate." Glancing at Bridget, she added, "We'd better look into the cat colony. Winters come in hard in hill country, Ivy."

"I grew up here, remember?" I said. "That's why I mentioned it."

"Is that tone?" Cori brushed back her Audrey Hepburn hair with more orange middle finger on display than strictly necessary. "Maybe you'll throttle that back when you see what we have to show you."

She leaned over and pulled a tablet out of the backpack at her feet. Pulling off a glove, she cued something up. Meanwhile, I looked around the circle and realized from the curious expressions that whatever Cori had to show me, only Bridget had already seen. Her black dog, Beau, leaned into her to offer comfort and her fingertips found his feathery ears.

That made me nervous. If Bridget needed Beau's help to get through this revelation, it couldn't be good. She'd seen some terrible things in her Mafia work, and was no shrinking violet.

My throat was bone dry by the time Cori handed me the tablet. Jilly leaned in and Keats left Cori to wedge himself between us, mumbling something under his breath. Staring at the screen, I tried to get my bearings. The image was steady but dark. It took me at least 30 seconds to realize I was watching my own henhouse.

I looked up at Cori. "You guys have a spy cam on my henhouse?"

She shrugged. "Hannah set up cameras everywhere but we turned them off until this little problem of yours arose."

"Which problem in particular?" I asked.

"The murder problem," Cori said. "Do you want to talk or watch?"

I lowered my eyes. There was movement on screen now. It looked like someone was placing an aluminum ladder against the coop.

"When was this?" I asked.

Jilly gestured to the bottom corner of the screen. "This morning at six. Right after you left the coop, I'm guessing."

"Bingo," Cori said. "We edited you out to get to the good stuff."

On screen, someone in baggy camouflage—pants, jacket, and a hat with earflaps—was climbing the ladder carefully, gripping it with black gloves.

"Is it a man or a woman?" Jilly asked.

"Skinny man?" I guessed. "Human scarecrow?"

"All shall be revealed," Cori said, clearly relishing every moment. "This really is worth the watch, so please be patient."

When the intruder reached the large, screened window over the door, he or she pulled something out of their pocket and sliced into the wire mesh. The knife slid around three sides of the window easily, and then the intruder pressed the wire up, back and out of the way.

Two more steps up, and the intruder was able to lean into the henhouse with a flashlight. The confident, efficient movements made me think it was a man, especially when he didn't hesitate before raising a leg to climb inside. He might not have been nervous but I held my breath, despite knowing there was shelving on the other side to provide stable footing. With only a modest amount of wriggling and squirming, the intruder managed to get the other leg inside, brace himself with gloved hands, and back inside the coop. Now he was more or less facing the camera but the henhouse eaves threw darkness over him.

I gripped the tablet harder and grunted in frustration.

"Patience," Cori said, her voice filled with suppressed glee.

Just as the intruder on screen was about to disappear completely, he hit his head on the upper ledge and exclaimed, "Dagnab it."

I gasped as I recognized that voice.

"What?" Jilly said. "Who is it?"

"Keep watching," Cori said. "The reveal is nigh."

Sure enough, as I tapped the screen to zoom in, the person's camouflage hat flipped off and tumbled to the ground outside the henhouse. For just a second or two before the head withdrew into the henhouse, Jilly and I got a very good look at our intruder.

And her perm.

───────

CORI HAD EDITED the video so that it only took a minute or two more for us to watch Edna Evans climb back out of my henhouse. She descended the ladder with relative ease, stooped to pick up her hat, and then carried the ladder around the barn to where Charlie usually left it.

And just like that, she was gone.

"You gotta give it to her, she did great for eighty. Dagnab it," Cori said, chuckling. "But why on earth was Edna Evans climbing into your henhouse?"

"More importantly, why on earth isn't Edna dead?" I asked. "If she's alive and fit enough to climb into my henhouse, who exactly is down at the county morgue right now?"

"That's a very good question," Bridget said, at last. "You saw her, right? After what happened? I mean, up close?"

"Very close. It was definitely Edna Evans, and she was definitely dead. I was still there when the paramedics pulled her out and confirmed it." I glanced helplessly at Jilly. "We'd spent enough time together recently for me to know."

"And yet here she is," Cori said, taking the tablet from me and handing it to Remi. The others crowded around to watch.

"You're sure the time stamp is correct?" Jilly asked.

Cori nodded. "We doubled checked it and dropped by to inspect the camera. I only wished we'd turned on the interior hen cam. I wanted to, but the others said you were a little touchy about our vigilance."

"I was. I am." I shrugged. "At the same time, I'm grateful."

"We just feel such an obligation to Hannah," Bridget said. "And when you mentioned someone had tried to break into the henhouse the other day we thought it couldn't hurt to have a lens on it."

"I wish you'd turned on the inside lens, too," I said. "I'd love to know what undead Edna was doing in there."

"Undead Edna," Jilly repeated. Her shoulders started shaking and then she giggled.

Suddenly we were all laughing. I felt a mixture of disbelief, relief, and a whole lot of confusion.

Finally, I took the tablet back so that I could watch undead Edna perform a stunt many women half her age would find challenging. "I'm—I'm stunned." It was all I could think of to say. "I don't know what to make of it."

"Put Ivy out of her misery, Cori," Bridget said. She was fighting a smile but her fingers were still on Beau's head.

"After we saw this today," Cori said, "I visited an old friend, Clarence Dayton."

"From one of the founding families of Dorset Hills?"

Cori raised delicate swallow eyebrows in surprise and approval. "Correct. I suspected he might know the Evans family, and sure enough, he did. He told me about the fire that decimated the family home when Edna was around fifteen. Her twin sister was killed in the fire. Or so he thought... until today."

My head hurt with the flood of new information, and I looked down at Keats to ground myself. His head tipped a little to offer me his brown eye—the eye of comfort and stability. It only took a moment till the tightness in my chest released and I could breathe more easily.

"So the woman in the pig pool was Edna's twin?"

"Probably," Cori said. "Her name was Agatha, according to Clarence Dayton."

"Probably?" I said.

"Well, I suppose it's possible that Agatha also has a perm and she's the one climbing into your henhouse."

"I guess. But it seems more likely that Edna was visiting her hens. She's very fond of a silky bantam named Sookie." Looking at Keats again, I added, "Now that I think about it, Keats was oddly detached when we found the body. He loved going over to Edna's and I would have expected more of a reaction to her passing."

"You never know how a dog is going to react to a death," Cori said.

"Unfortunately, I know how this dog reacts to a death," I said. "I should have watched him more closely. He always gives me clues. Always."

Cori nodded. "He's a pretty amazing dog, I'll give you that. Next time, pay attention."

"There had better not be a next time," I said.

"Agreed," Jilly said. "My big question is, why did Edna essentially fake her own death?"

"My first guess was that she poisoned her sister and went on the lam," Bridget said.

"Or maybe someone else killed Agatha by accident, thinking it was Edna," I suggested. "And now Edna's afraid she'll get framed for it. I would be."

"That'd be my guess," Cori said. "If so, she'll lie low till the real killer shows themselves."

"The truth always comes out," Jilly said. "At least it has so far."

"It needs to come out sooner rather than later," I said. "Because it seems like someone desperately wanted Edna gone. If they find out she's still scaling buildings, they'll likely strike again."

A shudder ran around the entire circle and Keats shook himself, his tags jangling. Beau followed suit, and then Leo did the same.

"And that person may be staying under your roof right now,"

Bridget said. "I'm sorry to say that but I worry about you. And the animals."

"I know, and I understand," I said.

"If you want my advice," Cori said, "and who wouldn't? I'd get that brilliant dog of yours working for his kibble. Do you hear me, Keats?"

He ran over to her and gave her a mumble.

"Huh," I said. "He usually only talks to me."

"Oh, we understand each other," Cori said. "And he's telling me you need to get your butt in gear."

CHAPTER SIXTEEN

I sat shivering on our usual stone bench in Clover Grove Gardens, waiting for Kellan to arrive. At least it was our usual meeting place 15 years ago, and we'd used it again recently. I'd hoped our visits would become a regular thing again by now, but on this blustery late October day, it seemed more likely that wouldn't happen till spring. Kellan and I might be closing the gap between us, but it was at approximately the same pace of the snail Keats was trying to herd across the stones toward the rusty orange chrysanthemums.

"Everything worthwhile takes time, buddy," I said, as he poked at the snail with his nose. "We need to remember it's a long game. Patience is not our strong suit."

I sighed, realizing I was picking up terms the Bridge Buddies tossed around. At this point, I could only assume one of them had intended to kill Edna Evans but had ended Agatha's life instead. And if Edna was going to sneak around in camo gear, it was only a matter of time before someone saw her and the stories started circulating. Then, either the killer would get to her, or the hill country winter would take her first. Edna might be as tough as a cockroach but she was still an octogenarian.

Keats gave up on his herding and delicately picked up the snail. With his tail high, he carried it the last few feet and placed it in the flower bed. Then he gave a mumble of disgust to let me know his sacrifice had come at a cost to his taste buds.

"Good for you," I said. "You're a hero to creatures great and small."

His prance of pride quickly transformed into a stiff stalk and he dropped to his belly. Before I could even turn, he charged across the garden and circled Kellan with unbridled joy.

"Is that dog happy to see me, or just happy to have a victim?" he called. Walking briskly, he kept a wary eye on his black-and-white blur, who was dodging and weaving as he delivered Kellan to me.

"You're a big step up from the snail he was just herding," I said, grinning. "I hope you're flattered."

"Very much so. But if he punctures these cuffs, I'm cuffing him and holding him on assault charges."

"Keats," I said, seriously for once. "Stand down on the chief. You know we can't afford silly distractions today."

"No?" Kellan joined me on the bench. His smile wasn't smouldering like the other day but it was almost better: friendly. Authentic. He was happy to see me. What a shame I had to ruin the mood with talk of murder. "If you're telling Keats to behave, then it must be serious indeed."

"It is." Taking a deep breath, I blurted, "I've just learned that Edna Evans isn't dead, after all."

I expected shock. Consternation. Or at least the confusion I'd felt earlier. Either Kellan had a way better poker face than I did, or the revelation didn't come as a huge surprise.

"You know this for a fact?" he asked, simply.

"Unless the zombie apocalypse has arrived in Clover Grove, I'm quite certain she was very much alive and well this morning as she climbed a ladder and broke into my henhouse."

That did surprise him. His blue eyes widened and his brows rose. "She went in through the window? That's ambitious."

"Kellan Harper! You knew she wasn't dead and didn't tell me? That's terrible!"

"I didn't know and I still don't know for sure," he said. "I only suspected. And a police chief doesn't share suspicions till he has evidence."

I handed him my phone and he watched the video, shaking his head pretty much continuously. "Wow. That woman is something else," he said, when it ended. "But we don't know for sure it's Edna Evans."

"Here's what I know," I said. "Edna had a perm the day before the event at my inn. So unless her doppelgänger has the same fresh perm, that's Edna."

"The woman in the morgue doesn't have a perm," he said. "At least so far as I understand what that is." He reversed the video. "Tight curls, right?"

"Correct. Her hair was too drenched for me to notice at the time. So then we need to assume Edna's twin sister, Agatha, is the one who ran into trouble at the pig pool."

"Not necessarily," Kellan said, basically confirming he knew about Edna's twin. "How do we know it wasn't Agatha who got the perm? It's quite common for twins to pass themselves off for one another, isn't it?"

"Not at eighty," I said. "Youthful pranks, yes."

"I suppose few have the motivation or opportunity by the time they reach that age," Kellan said. "But that doesn't mean it didn't happen here."

"I spent many hours with the permed twin the day before the murder and I can say with confidence that it was the real Edna Evans. Perm twin was able to cite my history and flaws with ease." I made a face. "Only someone who knows me well could be as mean and hurtful as she was that day."

"Or Agatha's just a very good actor, who's learned her lines and nailed her sister's caustic style."

"Question *my* judgement if you like, but Keats would know the difference. For reasons that elude me, he actually likes Edna. She gives him a subtle kick or two every time he's there but he's decided it's a game."

It was weird to be talking about Edna in the present tense again, but I had to adapt.

"Everything's a game to Keats," he said. "But it's only fun until someone breaks a hip."

"It's her choice to kick my dog and climb into my henhouse," I said. "I'd rather she come home and face the music. Because someone's got it out for her and knocked off the wrong sister."

Finally his expression grew serious. "Probably true, although we're still waiting on confirmation. It takes advanced testing to discern identical twins. We should know tomorrow."

I glared at him. "I still can't believe you didn't tell me. I'd like to point out that I called you immediately when I found out."

"Which is exactly what you need to do, as a civilian," he said. "I don't disclose information until the timing is right. And the timing definitely wasn't right. We don't have genetic proof one way or the other."

"We have a perm and a dog. That's proof enough for me."

He laughed out loud, and while I loved that sound—especially in that garden—I wasn't as receptive to it now.

"Ivy, that kind of thinking is exactly why I didn't tell you earlier. If you thought Edna was alive, you'd go looking for her. For reasons that elude me, you actually like her. Even though she gives *you* subtle kicks, just like Keats. And breaks into your henhouse."

"Very funny." I stared around the garden, pouting. There was little left to look at, with the first frost looming. The last floral stragglers seemed to be wrapping thin arms around themselves, knowing it was hopeless.

He patted my leg, and despite my annoyance, undeniable sparks lit up under the baggy denim. Traitorous leg.

"Look, I would have told you tomorrow when the results came back," he said. "I can't have you—or anyone else—running off looking for this woman right now. For all we know, it could be Edna's rather evil twin."

I turned quickly, losing the pout. "Is Agatha evil?"

"Well, evil's not a word I toss around lightly. But Agatha makes Edna look like a sweetheart."

I waited for him to say more, and when he didn't, I prodded. "Where's she been all this time? I heard she died in a house fire as a teen."

"That was the story, although police at the time didn't have our resources to confirm the identity of remains. It turns out Agatha escaped and spent the better part of her life in Australia, running petty scams and living off the generosity of her sister. There are records of payments going from Edna to an Australian account for sixty years."

"Why was she footing the bill for Agatha?"

He shrugged. "Unclear. Could have been hush money. Or maybe she just wanted Agatha to stay away. But people like Agatha are never satisfied. So she's come back a few times over the years to extract larger sums. I assume she made the long trek again recently to do the same."

"No wonder Edna has to live so frugally," I said. "She's been funding a freeloader all these years."

"We'll get the story from her—assuming it's her—when she surfaces."

"Why did she run? Do you think she killed Agatha?"

Again, he shrugged. "She's had plenty of opportunity before and chose to pay her off instead."

"So you think someone else tried to kill Edna and got the wrong twin?"

"It's possible that finally worked in Edna's favor. It's also possible that someone was after Agatha. She has enemies in Australia, and perhaps here, too. Maybe Edna was afraid of being framed for the crime. And she was right to worry."

"Well, this is frustrating," I said, getting up to pace, with Keats at my heels. "We need to find her and get some answers."

He got up, too. "You mean *I* need to find her and get some answers. You, on the other hand, need to attend to your guests and your livestock. Aren't you always telling me your animals are your top priority? Now that you know an evil twin may be stalking your chickens, you should be keeping a close eye on them."

"That's what the hen cam is for," I said.

He laughed again and this time I laughed with him.

"You finally set up the security cameras I asked you to get," he said.

"Actually, this footage came from Hannah's cameras."

His smile blew away in the chilly wind. "You got this from that band of lawbreakers, didn't you?"

"No comment. The cameras rightfully belong to me now. I've got eyes on all the animals, inside and out."

"Ivy, be careful with that crew. They seem to make their own rules in Dorset Hills, but I won't have that here." He rubbed a hand over his ruffled hair. "One rescue renegade wouldn't be so bad, but there's too many of them to keep track of."

"It is a big group," I said, keeping it neutral. "Backed by their mayor."

"Who's one of them," he said, rolling his eyes. "Or at least, she was. She knows how to bend the law pretty far, too."

I wished Kellan hadn't taken such a strong stance against the Mafia. While I hadn't deliberately become affiliated with them, I admired their work and was rather pleased to have a spot in their minor league.

"About Edna," I said. "Will you at least let me know when you find her? I'm worried."

He nodded grudgingly. "I know you are. But please remember that she may have murdered her own sister. Or vice versa. Only the tests will tell, and even then there's a margin of error with identical twins."

I had more faith in Keats, with his sharp nose and even sharper intuition. But I didn't press the point. I was already disappointed that Kellan and I were ending our meeting on a rather sour note after such a promising start. Next time I wouldn't sully our old meeting spot with business, since we often didn't agree on it.

"What about the Bridge Buddies?" I asked. "It seemed like there were scandals piled sky high among them."

"There always are in small towns. Maybe more than in big cities, actually." He turned and started walking. "I have some leads but there's no evidence that any of the scandals are current, or threatening to surface again. Any tensions simmering between these 'buddies' weren't bubbling too hard."

"They use bridge to keep it all locked down," I said.

"There are worse addictions," he said. "I've seen plenty."

I was quite sure he had, and again I wondered what had either lured or driven him back to Clover Grove. His work in Philadelphia had likely taken quite a toll on him. And now he was facing one crisis after another here. My annoyance ebbed a little. Obviously I wanted him to be happy, and more specifically, happy with me.

As we headed back to the parking area, Keats tried running a big loop to bring us together but this time, neither one of us fell for his sly tricks.

Gravel crunched under my boots as I offered one last observation. "Edna wouldn't be visiting Sookie if she were a murderer."

"And Sookie is...?"

"Her silky bantam. A sweet little hen who loves to be held and stroked."

"Ah." His brows managed to hoist themselves out of a glower to a normal position. "So you're still of the mind that animal lovers don't hurt people—despite firsthand experience it's untrue."

I sighed. "I really want it to be true. But I acknowledge there are exceptions to the rule."

He opened the driver's door to the pickup and managed to restrain himself from commenting on Buttercup's absence. Instead he focused on the matter at hand.

"My job is all about exceptions and rules, Ivy. If I didn't keep my eye on which is which, there would very likely be chaos. My role is to prevent chaos in Clover Grove."

I let Keats jump into the truck and climbed in after him "I know. And I appreciate that."

His gaze was so intense I had to look away. "Trust me," he said. "That's all I ask."

"I do." I rolled down the window as he closed the door. "Always have, always will."

A smile found its way back to his face. It was neither smouldering nor super friendly, but it was *something* and it would have to do.

CHAPTER SEVENTEEN

I always felt a little guilty about exploiting my brother's interest in Jilly, but when Kellan ordered Asher to spend the afternoon with us, it gave me a free pass. Whether Kellan was keeping a close eye on the Bridge Buddies or on me was unclear. Either way, Asher was much easier to dodge than the chief. He was crestfallen when Jilly told him she needed to run into town to replenish supplies but lit right back up when she said she'd bake him a blueberry buckle as soon as her kitchen was unpacked. I was pretty sure Asher had no clue what a buckle was—Mom had barely lifted a spatula in our youth—but he was ready, willing and able to enjoy anything Jilly prepared. Now that police had cleared her kitchen of any evidence of poison, and her culinary reputation had been restored, there were blue skies and bright smiles all around.

"I don't like pulling the wool over your brother's eyes," she said, as we headed down the lane in my truck. "How's he ever going to trust me?"

"Well, for starters, Asher trusts everyone. It's a bit of a disadvantage in his job, but a nice quality in a brother and boyfriend."

Jilly laughed. "He's not my boyfriend, and if I go sneaking around on him, he may never be."

"It's possible the sun will rise from the north tomorrow, as well," I said. "In fact, that's even more likely than my brother letting you get away."

"I hope you're right. We'll run into town for groceries to cover our butts, right?"

"Definitely. This won't take very long."

"That's what you always say. It's almost never true."

"I know. Have I mentioned how much I appreciate you yet today?"

"You have, but it's good to keep that on the front burner."

Keats didn't bother worming his way onto her lap. He was pacing across the back seat, looking more anxious than I'd ever seen him. Normally he was excited about a mission—any mission—but this one had him seriously rattled.

"It'll be fine, buddy," I said. "But if you want to sit this one out, I understand. Jilly's got my back."

That only made him pace faster. Keats and I had pledged a solemn oath to each other and he couldn't abandon his duty. But the steady panting told me it came at a cost.

"Should I be scared?" Jilly asked. "I mean, Keats is never scared. So I should probably be terrified."

"It's all good. Just in and out in less than an hour. We will assess the situation, notify Kellan about anything untoward and then make our way into town for supplies. Keats is being a drama queen."

I turned right, geared up smoothly and then turned right again into Edna's driveway.

"You're doing so much better in this thing," Jilly said. "My neck barely hurts now and the scratches on my legs from Keats trying to balance are healing nicely."

"Thanks," I said. "But don't jinx me. I think the truck just needed to be embarrassed into behaving by a yellow jalopy."

We parked around the back and jumped out of the truck. Both

of us were dressed in black—jeans, jackets, hats and gloves. Everything felt restrictive after months in baggy overalls, but I'd taken our cue from the Rescue Mafia.

Lowering the tailgate, I grabbed a large backpack. Inside, I'd packed a powerful flashlight, a coiled rope, a small hatchet, and handcuffs I'd found in an apartment I'd rented after college and kept around just in case. Jilly's backpack contained protein bars and a dozen tins of liquid meal replacement.

"I hope we don't need any of this," she said.

"Me too. I've got the bad twin covered with my bag, and you've got the good one covered with yours. Keep in mind that the hatchet and handcuffs can be used against us by either one."

We slid the straps of the backpacks over our shoulders and started walking to the trail. I ignored Keats skulking behind us, knowing he'd be even more ashamed if I drew attention to it. We were all entitled to our demons, and cats in swamps happened to be his.

"I'm sure we're capable of handling an old woman together," Jilly said. "Even if that woman is capable of scaling buildings."

"We can't let our guards down for a second," I said. "If she's there, she's probably gone a little bush crazy already. She must be terrified at the prospect of winter out here."

"I bet she has a ticket to Maui," Jilly said. "She's just waiting till the coast is clear to fly."

"Maybe. I doubt it though. She loves her house. She loves her creepy dolls and she loves her hens. Imagine starting all over at her age. Even in Maui."

"I know. But it's not safe for her to do any of the things she loves while her sister's killer is still at large."

"Now I understand why she was always surveilling with binoculars and night vision goggles. She had good reason to worry about her safety."

"If she's lived all those years in fear and frugality, it's no wonder she got so bitter," Jilly said.

"Once this is resolved she can have a peaceful life," I said. "But first we need to talk some sense into her. Kellan will make sure she's safe."

As we forged deeper into the bush, Jilly stared around and shivered. "For the record, I'm with Keats on this. I'm not big on cats and I'm definitely not big on swamps. If I fall in, you're going to owe me so big, Ivy."

"How could I owe you any bigger?" I said, squeezing her arm. "I'm already on the lifetime repayment schedule."

"It's a good thing I got my kitchen back. That goes a long way to even things out. No way I could ever in this lifetime afford a kitchen like that."

"And it would be utterly wasted on me, so it worked out well. I'll never bake Kellan a buckle, I'm afraid."

Jilly laughed and it was a comforting sound. "You have other assets he admires. When is that date happening?"

"Half past never at the rate we're going. But a girl can hope."

She gave me a sidelong glance. "If the girl hoped that much, she wouldn't stage sly expeditions behind Chief Hottie's back."

"A girl's gotta do right by her crabby old neighbor. Even if it comes at the expense of her love life."

"Are we there yet?" Jilly whined. "I wanna go shopping."

"Almost." I looked over my shoulder at Keats. He'd been following right on my heels but I wanted him to be free to watch for scary cats. "How ya doing, buddy?"

He was panting so much that his tongue was actually dripping. His muzzle swivelled left and right over and over, scanning for the dreaded colony of abandoned—or stolen—cats.

Finally we reached the clearing. Unlike the other one, it appeared completely empty. There were no cats sitting sentinel on the wall of Asher's old fortress. No cats tripping lightly over the crisscrossing highway of mossy logs. Nothing.

"Maybe she took all the cats and left," Jilly whispered. "Like a queen bee does with her hive."

"Possibly," I whispered back. "But I bet she's in the old clubhouse." I pointed across the pond. "Asher and his friends built that at least twenty-five years ago."

Jilly shook her head hard. "I'm not crossing the pond to get there. No way. Those logs look treacherous. Half of them are rotted out."

"Probably," I said. "I'll go alone. You and Keats stay here."

"I'm not letting you go alone," she said. "What kind of friend would I be?"

"The kind of friend who doesn't want to fall into a swamp?" I said. "Someone needs to be reasonable here. If something happens to me, you and Keats need to run back and get help."

Jilly looked down at Keats. "You staying?"

The poor dog looked as miserable as the day I found him in the criminal's yard. "Buddy, stay with Jilly. I mean it."

He gave me a quick trio of pants: no-no-no.

"If he's going, I'm going," Jilly said. "Besides, I'm just as scared to hang back here. What if the Queen Bee is out for a jaunt and comes back with the hive?"

"Good point," I said. "Alright, folks. Take it slow. Stay focused. Distraction is the enemy of balance."

I took my first tentative steps across a log.

"How deep is it anyway?" Jilly asked.

"Not very," I said. "It's the silty bottom you've got to worry about. Like quicksand."

"So reassuring," Jilly said.

"Just let yourself float to the surface and grab the nearest log. Easy peasy."

"Unless you're weighted down with a heavy backpack."

"Good point. Drop the pack and save yourself. If she wants it she can dive for it. I bet she has scuba gear out here. I think she's a prepper."

"Well, she was right about the zombie apocalypse," Jilly said. "You've got to hand it to undead Edna."

I stopped walking and raised my arms. "If you make me laugh, Jilly Blackwood, so help me dog I will drown you myself."

She held her arms out, too, and for a second, I really thought she was going to topple—first with hysterical laughter and then into the marsh. But then she remembered her own yoga-style lectures to me and took a couple of deep breaths.

"That was close," she said. "The rotting vegetation must be releasing laughing gas."

"Stop it, or you'll never be more than bush league Mafia. Think black ops, Jilly."

There was another snicker behind me and I came pretty close to losing it myself. But then something caught my eye. Flitting figures. Black, orange and white. I pointed as they ran off to the right into the bush.

"Should we follow them?" Jilly whispered.

"Decoys," I said. "Onward to the clubhouse."

We were two-thirds of the way there when the door flew back and the camouflage scarecrow darted out. Today she was wearing a balaclava, too. Without so much as a word, she hopped onto another log that ran parallel to us and started back across the pond on her very own highway.

"Edna, stop!" I yelled. She raised her hand, either for balance or a rude gesture. I didn't have the luxury of a leisurely assessment. "Turn back, Jilly."

Somehow I managed to pivot fully, grateful for the treads on my sneakers.

Jilly turned even more skillfully and said, "Go, Keats, go."

He was the slowpoke of the party. Despite being 10 times more agile than the two of us combined, it was like he was moving through thick tar. Nonetheless, we reached a log crossroads just in time to head Edna off at the pass. She turned back with surprising ease and started back toward the clubhouse.

What we didn't expect was the cats running interference. It was like they'd choreographed the whole thing beforehand. Dozens of them came at us from every direction, racing nimbly over every log. Their tails were aloft, like so many furry flags, suggesting they were actually enjoying their maneuvers.

"Keats, can you bark or something?" I said. "Fake it buddy, fake it."

He tried, but it was a weak, hollow-sounding wuff. Pitiful actually.

"Okay," I said. "I got this."

Taking a deep breath, I started running. I'd seen Asher do it long ago, just like a professional log roller. The worst that could happen was that I'd end up in the drink, and I'd been there before. But today I didn't slip. Instead, I almost danced across the last few yards like a cat myself. I looked back and urged Jilly and Keats on.

Meanwhile I kept an eye on Edna, who was beating it across the clearing literally surrounded by cats.

When Jilly and Keats touched down, I turned and ran after Edna, leaping over gnarly tree roots and squelching through puddles. She knew the terrain well and it almost seemed like the cats were leading her. Still, we gained on her. It was good to know that two thirty-somethings could still outrun an octogenarian, even carrying heavy backpacks.

"Fold your cards, Edna," I called, puffing hard. "The game is over."

She kept going, but the cats turned as one and surged back toward us with the black cat in the lead and Big Red and Fleecy right behind him. The others fanned out like a flock of geese. When they reached me, they split and kept going. All of a sudden there was yelping. They had Keats! I turned so fast I nearly smacked into Jilly.

"Back off," I yelled when I saw the three lead cats had surrounded Keats, all puff, hisses, and swiping claws. "Get off him right now. We are trying to help Edna." They ignored me, dancing at Keats sideways, letting out yowls that seemed to echo back from the distant hills. "Stop that racket right now," I said, heading back. "I've never hurt an animal in my life and I won't start now. But whatever you do to my dog, I'll do to Edna. Trust me, I've got claws too."

It was like a switch turned off suddenly. All the caterwauling stopped and the cats turned and raced after Edna. Keats came up to me and his tail started rising. His ears pricked. He was getting his nerve back.

"Okay, you guys," I said. "One last push."

We raced after Edna again. I hated that we had to do it, but I'd be lying if I didn't admit there was some small satisfaction in tag-teaming with Jilly and Keats to take Edna down. We were as gentle as we could be, but she was fighting and caterwauling like one of her feral cats. That she rolled into the water was entirely her own fault.

It might have been sweet icing on the cake, but unfortunately, I had to wade in, pull her out and restrain her. I didn't get to enjoy the moment as fully as I might have otherwise, but once she was cuffed and cursing, I felt pretty darned good.

CHAPTER EIGHTEEN

I waved a tin of the meal replacement in Edna's general direction. "How about a snack?"

We had tied her securely to a tree before Jilly skipped lightly across the log highway, escorted by a dozen cats, to collect Kellan and team to show them the way back in.

"And how do you propose I consume that?" she said. "Since you've trussed me up like a Christmas turkey?"

"I haven't taped your mouth yet. Yet. Just tip your head back and I'll pour it in."

"The day I let you feed me like an old lady is the day I depart this mortal coil," she said.

"You didn't move like an old lady, I'll give you that." I rubbed my arm where she'd struck me with her walking stick. "Now I know why we never found your cane."

"You should have just let me go," she said. "I can look after myself. Always have."

Her little roll in the swamp had added greenish brown muck like camouflage to her cheeks, and the tight curls that had become so contentious didn't have much spring left in them. Her eyes, so frighteningly sharp, seemed to have dulled. In that moment, I could almost believe it wasn't Edna after all, but her evil twin Agatha.

Luckily, Keats had no such doubts. Now that the cats had backed away to a respectful distance, his confidence was nearly restored, and he sat beside Edna with his tongue lolling. She'd never had a kind word to say to him or about him, and today she'd tried twice to give him her signature kick before I tied her ankles. But he saw something good in her, and if he did, I did.

"I know you can take care of yourself in normal times, Edna. But this is different."

"What do you know about anything, Ivy Galloway? You're a do-gooder who can't mind her own business."

"Guilty," I said, pacing. The dampness had penetrated to my core and I was trying to stay warm. "I'm going into the clubhouse to get you a blanket. You're going to catch your death." I started to walk away. "Poor choice of words."

"Stay out of there," she called after me. "That's my private sanctuary."

"My brother built that clubhouse, and he'd want me to go in there and get you a blanket."

"Oh, he'd want me to die out here in the cold. Your brother hates me."

"Asher doesn't hate anyone, but you can't blame people for being scared of you after the way you ran the school vaccination program. All chickens eventually come home to roost."

She muttered something unintelligible and I continued to the clubhouse.

Inside, I discovered Edna had prepared well, and likely over a long period, for an event such as this. The place was small but well built, considering the age of the boys who designed it. There was room only for a cot and storage. She'd added the shelving herself and stocked it with canned goods and plenty of water. In one corner were a couple of locked metal trunks. Maybe that's where she kept her crossbow and other weaponry.

When I came out with two blankets, she said, "Tell your dog to stop staring at me."

"Tell your cats to stop following me everywhere."

"They're not my cats. They just gathered after I started my work here. Someone had to feed them."

"Annamae and Gertrude said you stole their cats. My two barn cats are here, too."

"All arrived of their own free will. But they're yours now, since I'm obviously going to jail."

"Why would you go to jail?" I squatted in front of her. "Did you kill your sister?"

She gave one shake of her droopy hair. "No, but I probably should have decades ago. Aggie's been nothing but trouble since the day she came into the world 13 minutes ahead of me." Her throat worked and she coughed before continuing. "Our parents were what people today would call abusive. Harsh. Mean. Punitive. Aggie snapped one day and burned the house down with my parents and a hired hand inside. I wish I could say I was sorry about losing our family, but it was actually freeing—especially when Aggie fled to Australia."

"But she didn't stay gone," I prompted.

"Turned up every few years like a bad penny. Always wanting money. She found out about a mistake I'd made as a young nurse—a medication error that nearly killed someone—and that's when the blackmailing started. Doctor Grainer wouldn't have hired me had he known I'd covered that up. Once I'd become indispensable I came clean with him, and Aggie lost her leverage. But by that point she had a record of petty crimes in Australia and I just wanted her to stay gone." Edna's eyes met mine for a second. "All I ever wanted was a quiet, respectable life. Do you know how hard it can be to get that?"

"Yeah, I do." I'd had a quiet, respectable life in Boston, but in Clover Grove, it seemed like someone was always trying to snatch that away from me. "So then what happened?"

"What happened is that I worked myself to the bone with two and sometimes three jobs to keep Aggie comfortable. It was never enough because she gambled and made poor investments. Australia should thank me for boosting their economy."

I laughed and she gave a dry cackle, too.

"After I got pensioned out early from the school board, and Doc Grainer retired, I worked at Myrtle's Country Store. I was grateful to her for hiring me when no one else would. I needed the money to keep Aggie away. That's why I helped her out when the Lloyd situation came up. I didn't question why she wanted information. I had a debt to her."

"Ah," I said, relieved to know there was a reason she'd backed Myrtle McCain, who'd savagely attacked me once. "I'm sure Aggie wasn't happy being put on a budget."

"Oh no. But she hadn't made the trek back for a few years, and then she didn't collect my last few deposits. I hoped she'd died, not to put too fine a point on it. She didn't make the healthy choices I did." The dry laugh came again. "But she did inherit the cockroach survivor gene, and eventually turned up again." She glanced up at me. "I didn't know she was back till the day you told me you'd seen me near your henhouse. Since I hadn't been there, I knew my life was about to take a bad turn. And right before the bridge tournament, too."

"That's why you wanted to go home that night."

She nodded. "I knew she'd try to get in, and she had. She was sure I had some family jewels hidden away and wanted to make sure my will named her as beneficiary. To keep things simple, she said. When I didn't cooperate, she threatened to move to Clover Grove permanently. Can you imagine? What little social standing I had left would be decimated."

"And that's when you killed her?"

It was a sneak tactic that failed. "Nice try," she said with a withering glance. "Leave that sort of thing for your boyfriend when he arrives. I didn't kill Aggie. It was just one streak of good luck in my otherwise unlucky life. She came back early in the morning to try again. The greedy pig took the crème brûlée right out of my hand and had the audacity to eat it while trying to blackmail me. Then she 'borrowed' my shoes and left. Twenty minutes later I found her while walking to your farm. I put two and two together and came up with strychnine."

She raised her eyebrows and I shrugged a little.

"The poison was meant for me, of course, but I knew I'd be blamed. It probably even came from my old medical kit." She sighed. "So I came out here to ride things out. I was ready."

"Who really poisoned the crème brûlée?" I asked.

She gave a resigned shrug. "I trust you'll get that sorted out soon enough, Ivy."

"Me!"

"Well, you fancy yourself the new sleuth in town, don't you? You owe me this."

"I owe you something? Did I miss the huge favor you did for me?"

"It's more what I *didn't* do, like spread the word about Daisy and that dogcatcher. Plus there are stories about your other sisters you don't even know. Stuff that would tarnish your reputation even more were they to get out."

I glared at her. "So now you're blackmailing me."

Her eyes crinkled at the edges. I couldn't tell if she was serious or not. It could go either way with Edna.

"I don't need to blackmail you," she said. "You're going to do this anyway—for yourself and your farm and your family. I'll just benefit from that."

She was right, and I resented she could be so complacent about it. "Well I'd appreciate some leads, Edna."

"Miss Evans."

"Edna," I repeated. "Anyone who'd put me in this position forfeits the niceties. So just tell me who in Clover Grove would want you dead? And who is going to be really upset when they learn they pegged the wrong twin?"

"Honestly, Ivy." She sounded disgusted. "It would be easier to count who *wouldn't* want me dead. With Doc Grainer gone, I'm the repository of so many town secrets. People like the Bridge Buddies always care about reputation and they'll go a long way to protect it."

"Which one had most to lose?" I asked. "Gertrude? Morag?"

She shook her head. "You're going about this the wrong way. Let the police chief dig into the bridge club's tawdry secrets."

I got up and started pacing again. "Your secrets are pretty tawdry, Edna. Just saying."

"That's different." She had the decency to look a little sheepish, though.

"Maybe knowing what's different is the line that separates a sociopath from a regular flawed human being."

"Well, I never spilled their secrets. They just worried I might and that kept the balance of power. Although I could never for a single second let my guard down, and obviously I was right to worry. Maybe I'll finally get a moment's peace after you sort this out once and for all."

I checked my phone again. "Kellan will be here any minute to do just that."

"Let him work the official channels," she said. "You do it the other way."

"What other way?"

"The crazy way you and this dog work."

She nodded at Keats, who'd been sitting like a statue most of this time, staring at Edna with his cool blue eye. I was surprised he'd leave his back exposed to the feline army, but he seemed confident.

He flicked that blue eye at me now and I remembered what I'd wanted to ask her. "Right," I said. "I completely forgot about that! Thanks, buddy."

Edna shook her head. "That would be the crazy I was talking about."

"We don't have much time, Edna. Tell me what the little key was for."

"What little key?"

"The one in the curly doll's head." I could hear voices in the distance. "Hurry, now."

Her eyes had widened in horror. "How did you know about that?"

I nodded at Keats. "Crazy club, that's how. Was Aggie after what's behind that key? Does anyone else know about it?"

The drawstring pulled her lips tight but then she spit out, "That's personal. *Private.* It has nothing to do with anything. You put that key back where it belongs."

"Well, you've called on Keats to help and he thinks it has something to do with everything."

"Did you tell Kellan about that key?"

I blinked a few times. I'd meant to, and then I legitimately forgot about it until this moment. "I may have neglected to mention it," I said.

"Well, you can continue to neglect to mention it," she said. "Because it's personal. And private. One day you'll see why."

There was a growing clamour across the clearing and the cats scattered. My brother was the first to arrive and there was a grin on his face he couldn't suppress.

"See?" Edna said. "He hates me."

"He's just excited to be back here. Watch him."

Asher ran across the mossy highway like a veteran log roller and joined us. "You okay, sis?"

"Fine. We're both fine. Edna needs a lift over."

"I do not." Her indignation was palpable. "I've been preparing for this for years."

"She's turned your clubhouse into a bunker," I told my brother. "Prepping for the zombie apocalypse."

"That's what I built it for, Miss Evans," he said, untying her swiftly. "I'm glad you got to rise from the dead here."

"You're not funny, young man. I have plenty of needles in my trunk, you know."

Asher flinched but he didn't falter. Instead, he scooped her up and started back across the bridge.

Edna let her head drop over his arm to look back at me. "Find out who killed me, Ivy. Ask the cats."

"Ask the cats?" I called after her.

"That's what I said."

Asher's voice blared across the swamp. "She's delirious, Chief."

Edna argued with my brother the rest of the way, yet he never lost his balance. I waited with Keats, hoping they'd leave without me so I didn't get a similar lecture from Kellan. He waited, hands on hips, till I yelled, "I've got to talk to the cats. You heard the lady."

Panther was nowhere in sight but Big Red and Fleecy stared at me with eyes like saucers before slipping into the trees.

"We'll meet again, Keats," I said, giving up on them. "I'm sorry to tell you."

He gave a full body shake and then started back across the pond ahead of me, tail brushing the mossy logs. Like me, he probably felt our troubles were just beginning.

CHAPTER NINETEEN

The next morning I was up so early that I needed a flashlight when I walked around the barn to the henhouse. I shone the light up at the window Charlie had already screened and reinforced, and nearly jumped out of my skin. Staring down from the roof were six glowing eyes. I didn't need to see them clearly to know I was looking at Panther, Fleecy and Big Red.

"Just what do you think you're doing?" I called up to them. "I left plenty of kibble and water. You won't be getting fresh chicken for breakfast."

Six eyes blinked at me, eerie lights flashing off and on. Keats growled, a sound I heard rarely. I didn't know if it was a warning to me, or just annoyance that the three feline hooligans had invaded his turf.

"Go on now," I said, brandishing the flashlight at them. "I can't feed my chickens if you're trying to get in."

The eyes disappeared for a second as they looked at each other, consulting. Then they looked back at me, unblinking.

I remembered what Edna had said as Asher carried her off. *Talk to the cats.*

Well, I was barely a dog whisperer, and didn't know the first thing about communicating with cats, really. But no one was around, so it was worth a try.

"Edna wanted us to chat," I called up to them. "I'm open to a dialogue, because I know you guys were close." Their eyes all blinked at once, as if signalling an affirmative. "But I need that chat to happen in broad daylight. Nothing personal, but there are just too many politics." They turned in another apparent consultation. "I've got forty chickens to worry about," I said. "And you and my dog didn't get off to a great start. So let's meet again later, okay?"

The eyes disappeared suddenly and I had no idea where they'd gone. Maybe they'd circled behind me, waiting to dash into the henhouse when I unlocked the door.

"I can't chance it, Keats," I said. "We're going to have to leave the hens till Charlie gets here for backup."

He continued to growl as we walked back around the barn to do the other chores. "I know it's unnerving, especially when they can see us far better than we can see them. But if Edna wants us to make peace with them, we need to give it a try. You know as well as I do that fate works in mysterious ways."

His growl turned into a grumble of protest as I lit the barn and started the morning rituals. "Your pride took a massive hit, but you've got to adjust or it'll just bite you in the butt the next time. In this case, quite literally."

He followed me around a little too closely until I put him to work releasing the livestock. The only way to help an angsty sheepdog was to give him an important job.

Sure enough, once the goats, sheep and cattle were happy in their pastures, his tail was up and his ears were pricked. He was ready to embrace our next adventure, which just happened to be waiting for us in Dorset Hills.

I didn't bother going back to the house before climbing into the truck. "I'll grab another coffee at The Puccini Café," I said. "Last night took it out of me and I need to be quick on my feet for this meeting."

Keats put his paws on the dash and mumbled agreement.

"Exactly. It's time to sink our teeth into this mystery and get it solved. Like Edna said, it's personal."

He turned before I started the truck rolling and offered his white paw in a high five.

MERLE RANDALL MUST HAVE BEEN A VERY handsome young man, because he still cut a fine figure as he gave me a tour of the Riverdale community in Dorset Hills. His dignity was somewhat undermined by the two assertive and vocal dachshunds that pulled every which way at the ends of the leashes in his hand. Meanwhile, Keats stuck to my side on a loose leash I only used for appearances.

"I just can't believe how obedient that dog is," Merle said, shaking his white head. "These two really belong to my wife and they're impossible."

"I can't take much credit for Keats," I said. "It's the breed. Border collies practically train themselves."

"Helen spoils ours," he said. "They're her babies, now that our daughter and even granddaughter don't need us much anymore. In fact, our granddaughter is getting married soon."

"Congratulations," I said. "Well, I don't want to keep you too long, Mr. Randall."

"Merle," he said. "No one calls me mister anymore."

I smiled. "Well, I'm old school. As I said on the phone, I just wanted to have a quick word about Edna Evans. I'm speaking at her funeral and hoped to get a bit more background. I know you were old friends."

His face reddened and my own warmed in sympathy. It felt

wrong to make an old man blush, especially when I couldn't be fully honest about my mission.

"I was sorry to hear about what happened," he said. "She didn't deserve that. Edna was a proud woman and it would have embarrassed her greatly to end up in a..."

His voice drifted off, so I supplied, "Puddle." The marsh was a menacing waterhole but there was no use distressing him further.

"She could stop a clock back in the day," he said. "Half the men in Clover Grove fancied her, but I got her."

We stopped in front of a bronze statue of what looked like a Cairn terrier. The ratting dogs tended to run together for me, especially in bronze.

I waited for him to continue and eventually he did. "Edna was as sharp as a tack. Always laughing. She loved to dance—in fact, she never sat one out." He gave me a smile. "We had a lot of fun."

It was hard to believe we were talking about the same person. At least Edna had retained her quick wit and fitness.

"You were engaged for a while, or so I'm told."

Now his color deepened to maroon and he stared at the two wiener dogs, who were squabbling since they couldn't get him moving. "I intended to spend the rest of my life dancing with Edna. But her sister, Agatha, ruined everything."

That I hadn't expected, but I could dance, too. "Edna had a sister?"

"Oh yes. A twin who was supposedly identical, but Agatha was dark where Edna was light." He started walking again and the wiener dogs resumed their pulling and yapping. "When we met, Edna told me her twin had died in a fire that claimed the whole family. Unfortunately, just a month before we married, Aggie surfaced and played the oldest trick in the twin book: she pretended to be Edna and then sweet-talked me into lending her three thousand dollars to cover an old loan. Of course, I gave it to her without question, and when I mentioned it later, the whole thing blew up. Edna was furious I'd fallen for the ploy, and I was furious she lied about Aggie. Now we didn't have money for a wedding, even if we'd wanted to go through with it."

"Did you?" I asked. "Want to go through with it?"

He shook his head. "Not then. My pride wouldn't allow it. Edna started repaying me right away. It took years, but she did it—with interest. Meanwhile I met Helen not long after." He stopped in front of the next statue, a mere half block away, and sighed. "It was too soon. Remind me what you young people call that?"

"Rebounding," I said, with a smile.

"Exactly. I wanted to move on to prove I could. Helen and I married and had Sarah, our daughter, within the year." He met my eyes. "Don't get me wrong. Helen and I have had a good life, and Sarah, and now her daughter, are my pride and joy. But I sometimes think of what could have been if I hadn't been so proud."

"I understand pride, too," I said. "It's very tough to swallow without some time to season it. But if it helps, Merle, I know for a fact that Edna had regrets, too. The day before she, uh—" I struggled with the word and couldn't say it. "The day before the puddle incident, she told me you were the love of her life. I didn't know about Aggie. She just said she'd decided to focus on her career because no one else could compare."

"Ah." His eyes brightened. "I guess that's why she wouldn't give the ring back. Maybe in her mind it still connected us."

"She kept the engagement ring?"

He nodded. "It was a family heirloom. A huge diamond that's worth a bomb, in my wife's words. My mother never let up on it, and it became a sticking point. Helen is mad to this day that I didn't reclaim it—not so much for the value as for the symbolism."

"She felt like a secondhand rose," I said.

"That's exactly the term she used. And when she heard Edna passed, she wanted me to try to get it back through the estate so that my granddaughter can have it for her wedding. It's what my mother would have wanted, I know that. But I can't do it. In my day, a man showed honor by keeping his commitments. I was always ashamed of breaking the engagement and tradition said the woman could keep the ring."

"Maybe you liked having that tie as well," I said, smiling.

"Maybe." He sighed. "I'm ashamed to say that. It feels disloyal to my wife."

"It stays between us, I promise." I led him back the way we'd come. "Merle, is there any chance your wife would have tried to get that ring back on her own?"

"Helen? No. She's in a wheelchair now." He gestured toward the dogs. "That's why I'm on leash duty."

"What about Sarah or your granddaughter?" I asked. "I'm sure they'd love the ring for her wedding."

"Actually, my granddaughter said she'd refuse to wear it if she had it. I think she knows what it signifies and would feel disloyal to Helen. So Edna's heirs are welcome to it. Someone will inherit a lovely ring and a couple of nice pieces she got from her mother. Unless she pawned them to keep Aggie afloat." His mouth puckered in a way that resembled Edna's. "That would have always been a sticking point between us. I assume Aggie went back to Australia and stayed there, financed by Edna. I never heard her name mentioned again."

"Good riddance to bad garbage," I said.

"Exactly." He looked around. "I left Clover Grove for Dorset Hills to escape the shame and embarrassment, and I've done well here. It's turned into a circus now, but I always loved dogs so I've adjusted." We got to my truck, parked well away from his house, and he stopped. "Edna hated dogs and all pets, actually. So maybe things worked out just as they should have."

I let Keats into the truck and rolled down the window. "Merle, you wouldn't have Sarah and your granddaughter if you'd reconnected with Edna. She got the ring, you got the real jewels."

When I got in and closed the door, and looked out, Merle was beaming. "I like you, young lady. You could stop a clock too, if you don't mind an old man saying so."

Laughing, I smoothed the bib of my overalls. "I'm pleased to hear it."

"And take it from the same old man... don't ever let pride get in the way of true love. You don't want to end up my age with that kind of regret. It's a heavy load to carry."

I reached out and he squeezed my hand. "I wish I'd had a dad or granddad like you, Merle."

Now he flushed again, and this time, I didn't feel guilty at all.

CHAPTER TWENTY

Jilly had completely unpacked the kitchen and was up to her elbows in flour as she kneaded bread dough for a homemade pizza night. She had rarely looked happier than she did in that moment, which may have had something to do with Asher's plan to come and personalize his own pizza. I'd tipped her off to his topping combo: chopped dill pickle, pineapple and bacon. The man was going to be in heaven, particularly when he followed that zesty mouthful with blueberry buckle.

"You're sure you won't invite Kellan?" she asked. "It would be such fun."

"It's no fun if he's lecturing me. I want to enjoy my pizza, not defend our successful black ops mission."

"Well, he's not wrong. It was reckless and could have gone far off the rails."

I glared at her. "Whose side are you on?"

"The same side as my best friend, like always. Why do you think I was out there being reckless with you? You didn't even need to twist my arm."

"True." I scooped up shredded cheese out of a big bowl and

dropped it into my mouth. "Why does shredded cheese taste so much better than sliced?"

She slapped my hand away, dusting my sleeve with flour. "Some mysteries are better left unsolved."

"I bet shredding unleashes the flavor molecules," I said, trying to sneak around her and getting smacked with a spatula for my trouble.

"How about you just give your brain the night off and spend some quality time with your guests? You've barely been around the past few days."

"Like they'd notice. All they do is play round after round and then sleep."

She smiled. "They'll probably be the lowest maintenance guests we'll ever have. No one said a word of complaint about catered food. Tonight, I want to give them something they'll remember."

"No one will forget your homemade pizza. I'm quite sure of that."

I showered again before dinner. Despite having a shower both last night and in the morning, I still smelled of swamp. Somehow that short wrestle in the shallows with Edna clung harder than my dump a few days earlier. The murky algae still growing along the pond's edges wouldn't die till the first real frost. I'd be there to witness that happen because someone had to feed Edna's colony, at least until the Rescue Mafia could trap them and find enough shelters. It would be a long operation.

Meanwhile, Edna herself had been trapped and was in a shelter of Kellan's choosing. He refused to say where and I didn't particularly care, as long as she was safe.

When I came down for dinner, the usual calm that hung over the family room like a weighted blanket had disappeared. Gertrude and Morag were glaring at each other over their hands of cards and

Annamae was fanning herself with her cards. She pulled out her embroidered handkerchief to have it at the ready.

"What's going on, folks?" I asked. "Usually you could drop a pin in this room and hear it roll."

Gertrude and Morag didn't shift their gaze from each other or say a word, so I raised my eyebrows at Annamae.

"Morag thinks Gertrude peeked at her hand under cover of a cough," Annamae said. "I'm sure that's not true."

"Oh, it's true, and it's not the first time, either," Morag said. "Once a cheater, always a cheater."

Gertrude threw down her hand with a dramatic flourish. "There. Satisfied? I forfeit the game."

"You forfeit because you were going to lose," Morag said. "So no, I'm not satisfied."

"That's a little premature, isn't it? Normally I kick your butt, Morag Tanner," Gertrude said.

"Only because you have a better hired hand than I do." Morag tossed a hostile glare at her paid partner, Kimberly.

"Don't be rude to our support team," Gertrude said. "If you're oversensitive to losing, that's your problem."

"I'm oversensitive to cheaters," Morag said. "That's *your* problem."

Joan and the hired hands eased their chairs back, but Annamae held her ground, albeit while patting her eyes.

I thought about diverting the conversation into safer channels but decided to let the argument run its course. Flaring tempers could go interesting places.

"Old grudges certainly die hard, don't they?" Gertrude said. "This one's been eating away at you for decades. Anger can kill you, Morag."

"Well, it hasn't yet and I'm nearly eighty. I thought guilt and shame might kill *you* by now, but no such luck."

"Guilt and shame?" Gertrude's voice thundered and she rose from the table. "Why should I be ashamed? I didn't deliver an illegitimate child and put it up for adoption. I believe that was your daughter."

"Who had an affair with your husband. That you knew about and hid. Which makes you a cheater too, in my view."

Jilly came in from the kitchen just in time to see Gertrude sweep her cards right off the table. I signalled my friend to stay quiet as the cards fluttered to the hardwood floor.

"I made a choice to ignore my husband's dalliances," Gertrude said. "For the sake of family peace. I didn't condone them, obviously. I just looked the other way. I was never certain he and your daughter kept company... until now. It's unfortunate, but she was an adult, Morag. She made her own choices."

"We were friends." Now Morag did the thundering. She made an even more dramatic gesture to sweep off her cards, accidentally clipping Kimberly in the chin. "Friends don't do that to each other."

Gertrude crossed her arms. "Pish posh. We were never friends, any of us. We play bridge to keep an eye on each other. Your son forced my son out of business by spreading word he'd had a heart attack at thirty-seven. No one trusts an investment advisor who might pop off at any second."

"It's not my fault your son got bad genes from his heartless father."

"There was no heart attack. He had a bowel fissure that he was too embarrassed to share publicly. Men and their stupid pride! He preferred to let your son's slander ruin him."

"Ladies, really," Joan finally chimed in. "This is unseemly. You'll shock our hosts."

"What will shock our hosts is hearing about that stunt you pulled on your husband," Gertrude said. "Locking him out of the bedroom and inviting his brother in. Didn't he wonder about where the stork found your last child?"

"Stop it, all of you," Annamae said, sobbing now. "We *are* friends and friends don't behave like this." She got up to leave the room. "Enemies don't even behave like this."

"Oh, run away like you always do, Annamae," Gertrude called after her. "If you think we don't know about *your* husband's peccadilloes, you're wrong. He passed along a little problem, didn't he?"

Annamae gasped. "Edna told you!"

Gertrude gave a nasty little laugh. "She didn't need to. Our husbands spent time in the same disreputable company."

Morag circled the table and approached Gertrude. "Are you saying your husband exposed my daughter to something dangerous?"

She raised her hand, palm open, and I had no doubt she intended to slap the living daylights out of Gertrude.

"Ladies, that's enough," I said. "My brother will be here any second and I'll have you both arrested if there's any violence on my property."

Morag gave me a pleading glance. "Just one slap. I've wanted to do it for forty years."

"Do it," Gertrude said. "Then I'll drag what's left of your name through the Clover Grove gossip mill. We have plenty of witnesses."

"Fine with me," Morag said. "Because I've already let it leak you poisoned Edna."

Gertrude gasped. "You didn't!"

"I saw you in the kitchen looking at the crème brûlée," Morag said. "You left in a hurry when I caught you."

"That's a lie!"

"Your word against mine," Morag said. "One of us has a lying, philandering husband she's been covering for all these years. You live a lie."

"One of us has a grandchild she disowned," Gertrude said. "So Edna had as much to hide about you as me. And it so happened that I also saw you examine the crème brûlée with interest. You were holding a syringe at the time."

The women fell silent, staring at each other with such ferocity that none of us noticed we had a new audience. There was clacking on hardwood and a sudden clap that made everyone jump.

My mother stepped right in between the warring women and said, "Well, I got here just in time. A little bird told me some bridge players needed manicures, and I came prepared."

She lifted a large black bag that no doubt held an entire spa. Iris was behind her, wide eyes confirming they'd heard much of the argument.

Asher came in with his usual bright smile. "How's it going, folks?"

Gertrude and Morag both looked down at the same moment and Mom said, "Well, son, we're having a spa night for the ladies, so you'd be better to spend your time in the kitchen."

"Sounds good to me." He directed the full force of his smile at Jilly, who was wringing her apron in the kitchen doorway.

"I'm heading out for some fresh air," I said. "It's time to turn the manure. If you wait too long, it explodes."

CHAPTER TWENTY-ONE

M y nerves settled the second I walked into the barn. Simple, mindless chores were exactly what I needed to cleanse my soul from the mudslinging inside. I went out to unlock the gates to the sheep, goat and cow pastures and put Keats to work. He was able to open the gates himself at the right time if I left them unlatched, but still shut.

Back inside, I pulled out my phone to call Kellan. That's when I noticed three sets of eyes looking down at me from the loft.

"I see you're making yourselves right at home," I told Panther, Fleecy and Big Red. "Can I get you anything? The cat kibble is over at Edna's, but there's tinned tuna in the pantry if you can hang on for a bit."

At first there was no reaction, but one by one the cats came down to sit on a shelf and stare at me from close range. I put my phone on the shelf and my hands on my hips.

"Look, I don't speak feline," I said. "If you want to tell me something, you're going to have to be more explicit."

Big Red batted my phone off the shelf and before I could retrieve it, Panther jumped down and made a show of scraping loose hay over it with his front paw, as if covering excrement.

"That's not very nice, considering I just offered you hospitality."

Fleecy and Red jumped down too and they made a game of batting my phone around like a catnip mouse.

"Stop that." I darted in to get it. "Do you have any idea how much these things cost?"

I slipped the phone into my front pocket just as Keats brought in the sheep. He did a double take when he saw the cats—three in a row, backs arched and hissing. To give him full credit, he stayed focused on the task at hand.

Once the sheep were locked up, however, he took a little run at the cats and scattered them. Big Red leapt right over the dog and swatted at Keats' tail when he landed. He must have spared the claws or I'd have heard about it.

"Listen up, all of you," I said. "I like fun and games as much as the next gal, but when it comes to my livestock, I'm all business. So you three... Out of the way until Keats gets everyone to bed. If you want to behave like fools after that, go to town."

I wanted to believe the cats understood me because they jumped back on the shelf. But I think it had more to do with the prospect of more and bigger hooves coming their way. They weren't stupid, that much was obvious.

After opening the door to the goat pen for Keats, I pulled my phone out again. That's when all three cats started yowling in unison.

"Ah. *Now* I get it. You don't want me chatting to the police chief." I lowered the phone and the caterwauling stopped. "Right. But here's the problem: the chief insists on hearing every little detail about everything and if I don't share, I'm in big trouble. Believe it or not, he wants the best for Edna, as we all do."

They looked at each other, and one by one, started licking their front paws. I took that as tacit permission to carry on, and when I pressed Kellan's number, there was no further disruption.

When he picked up, I put him on speaker so that my hands were free to dish out the evening rations. "I've got one heck of a tale for you about the bridge club," I told him. "But first, I want to know how Edna—"

The caterwauling began again instantly. It was hard to believe three small creatures could create such a racket.

"What on earth was that?" Kellan asked, when they took a breather.

"Three cats followed me home from the marsh," I said. "They were sitting on the henhouse this morning, and now they've apparently moved into the barn."

"How's Keats taking that?" Kellan asked. "He didn't look pleased about the feline situation last night."

"Fur's going to fly if they decide to stay. But they'll need to work it out. I can't turn away Edna's—"

The caterwauling started again, like flicking on a light switch. This time I put two and two together. But first I had to test my theory. I waited for them to simmer down and said, "I might have to call you back when I've finished in the barn, Kellan. Because I have something really important to tell you about Ed—"

I didn't even get both syllables out before the cats started their vocal gymnastics. This feline security team did not want me saying Edna's name out loud. At least, not here.

"Got it," I said, saluting them.

"Got what?" Kellan asked.

I didn't want to tell him I was communing with cats now, so I just said, "Let's chat later."

"How about I come over there when I'm done in an hour?" he said.

"Sounds good. On the upside, it's pizza night. On the downside, my mom's here doing manicures on the guests."

"Next idea," he said. "How about I pick you up and we head over to Bone Appetit Bistro in Dorset Hills?"

"Sure!" I must have sounded too eager because Fleecy let out a rather grating meow. Keats had just delivered the goats and after I closed the door behind them, he tilted his head and shot me a rather sweet look with his brown eye.

"All right then," Kellan said. "See you in just over an hour."

After I hung up and double checked to make sure we were disconnected, I told my audience, "It's not a date. The police chief just wants to hear my story without constant disruption."

The phone buzzed with a text from Kellan: "Keats isn't invited."

It was a date.

CHAPTER TWENTY-TWO

Jilly could hardly stay still long enough to run her flat iron through my hair. "Finally. I thought this day would never come."

"I don't know for sure it's a date," I said. The moment after his text, I'd begun to doubt. "We're going to a restaurant, so it makes sense not to bring Keats."

We were locked in Jilly's en suite bathroom, which was so packed with makeover options that Keats had to sit in the shower stall and watch.

Jilly turned to him now and asked, "Is it a date, Keats?" The dog offered a sloppy smile and gave three quick pants: yes-yes-yes. "See? I trust his instincts more than yours."

I gave a shrug of submission. "We were on speaker, so I suppose the dog's opinion has merit. Just the same, I don't want to look like I'm trying too hard, Jilly. Imagine if it's *not* a date? Then I'll feel stupid, because Kellan knows I don't fuss much with my hair."

"He doesn't know what you do with your hair when you go to restaurants, because you've never dined out since you got here."

"Why would I when the best chef in town is under the same roof?"

"Flattery will get you everywhere," she said. "Even into my lucky cashmere sweater, which I was going to wear myself later."

"Eww, no," I said, as she held up a sky-blue cardigan. "That sweater is intended for my brother. I'll take the next best option. Otherwise it's my gray jacket from the Flordale days."

Jilly was horrified. "You don't want to look like a suit with Kellan," she said, rifling through the pile of clothes she'd brought in.

"No buttons. Remember I popped Daisy's blouse and exposed my sports bra. Whatever you choose has to be low risk."

"You mean low cut," she said, tossing me a scoopy sweater in a mossy green.

"Too much like swamp," I said. "I have PTSD after last night."

"Compliments your eyes," she said. "And for pity's sake, change out of the sports bra and overalls. Tonight you're just regular Ivy, not farmer Ivy."

I checked my fingernails and saw the usual crescents of dirt. "I don't know regular Ivy anymore. She was last seen in college."

"Just relax. Have a glass of wine and watch your breathing. It's just Kellan, someone you already impressed long ago."

"Maybe I should have a couple of shots of Edna's vodka before we go."

"Absolutely not." She tipped my chin up and applied eyeliner with a steady hand.

"Enough," I said, as she dusted my face with loose powder. "Too much 'try.'"

"Ivy. Listen to reason. If you look fabulous, he's less likely to pull that 'I'm Chief Harper and you must comply' stuff and remember he's Kellan, the man who thinks you're a knockout."

"Good point. So I need to stun him with the straight hair and flutter the mascara so he forgets about yesterday's black ops mission."

"Exactly." She leaned in and sniffed. "No offence, my friend but I'm getting a whiff of swamp, mixed with a slight hint of—"

"Manure. I know, but there's no time for a third shower."

She spritzed me with her high-end perfume. "This will only mask it, so I suggest you keep a bit of distance. Save that steamy first kiss till next time."

"I can totally do that." I looked over at Keats. "How am I going to manage without my buddy tonight?"

"Get the shop talk over early and then just follow Kellan's lead. You can never go wrong by talking about the food, the scenery or the weather."

"I feel like I'm sixteen again. Only I wasn't this nervous back then."

"It's like learning to drive," Jilly said. "Imagine if you had to get your license now. You'd be terrified, whereas at sixteen you were charging down the highway, fearless."

"Good analogy," I said. "Too bad I'm a terrible driver."

THE BONE APPETIT Bistro was only moderately busy and there was a booth available by the window. I was grateful that the tables were wide because there was less chance of Kellan catching a whiff of my swamp-farmer bouquet.

"You look nice," he said, smiling.

I smiled back. "Good thing you gave me an hour after bringing in the herd."

"Keats took the bad news okay?"

"Surprisingly well. It helped that my mother was there. She's one of his favorites, as unlikely as it seems."

"That dog moves in mysterious ways," Kellan said, as a woman with a blonde bouffant came to the table with menus. "Maybe we should order before talking about what happened earlier."

I looked at the long list of items with kitschy Dog Town themed names and quickly settled on the Doggone Best Burger. Kellan chose the same. I didn't know if we did that out of expedience, or nostalgia for our high school favorite, Hills Hamburgers, but it kept things simple.

While we waited for the food to arrive, I told him about the dustup between Gertrude and Morag. He pulled out his notepad, and with every word he scribbled, it felt less like a date. A few frowns and a disgusted snort or two deflated my hopes for romance even further. I summed it all up in a few words. "They were accusing each other of murdering Edna, and threatening to annihilate each other's reputation in polite society."

"Lovely," he said. "Cutthroat small town politics at their finest."

"Do you think any of them did it?" I asked. "I mean, murdered Aggie by mistake?"

"Anything's possible. They all had access and it seems they all had motive. Some of those stories I knew, some I didn't." He closed his notepad with a firm snap. "And that concludes our business for the evening."

"Can I just ask if Edna—"

"Nope. You forfeited further details when you disobeyed my direct order to trust me to find her."

"I just went to feed the cats and one thing led to another."

"You went to feed the cats with a hatchet, rope and handcuffs?" He rolled his eyes. "Enough said about that. Let's talk about the weather."

I laughed. "The most popular topic in the farming community."

After that, I took Jilly's advice and followed his lead all the way through dinner. At one point I went on a bit too long about Heidi's mastitis, but noticed his glazed eyes and recovered pretty quickly. I was starting to feel almost comfortable, which was virtually unheard of for me now without Keats as a buffer. It struck me how dependent I'd become on my dog since his rescue. Getting out on my own occasionally was probably good for both of us. We were the very definition of codependent.

"What are you thinking?" Kellan asked. While I was lost in thought he'd leaned across the table.

I leaned in, too. "I was thinking about how nice this is. Thank you."

At close range, his smile was electrifying. His hand brushed mine on the table and there was a staticky spark that made me gasp. Kellan just smiled more.

I was quite sure he was going to kiss me right there in the restaurant, and I was going to let him, smell or no smell. If he liked me, he was going to have to get used to strange fragrances, odd noises and animal hair. He didn't seem terribly put off. In fact, he leaned in even more, and I... well, I followed his lead, just like Jilly ordered. The table was wide though, so it was getting just a tad awkward when a voice beside us said, "Ivy. Your—uh—chesticle is in the ketchup."

I sat back, startled, and glanced down before up. Cori Hogan was not wrong. Jilly's second favorite sweater and my nicest bra had a heaping helping of my favorite condiment. Kellan grabbed napkins, leaned over to help, and then stopped with his hand in the air.

"Yeah, I wouldn't," Cori said, grinning. "It's a G-rated restaurant."

"Cori, what are you doing here?" I asked.

"I come for the free fries." She pointed a gloved index finger at the counter. "Bridget's the manager here."

For the first time, I noticed Bridget pouring drinks and directing waiters. I guess I'd been too entranced to see her before.

"Kellan, this is Cori Hogan," I said. "She's the best dog trainer in Dorset Hills, from what I've heard."

"You heard right," she said. "And you're one of the few people who gets a passing grade for dog behavior without my intervention."

"Interesting," Kellan said. "Are you aware that Keats herds people and nips their uniform cuffs?"

She shrugged. "No dog's perfect. And if he nips your cuffs, officer, maybe it's because you need to be kept in line."

There was a tense moment between them. Or maybe it was only tense for me. Each of them had a little smile.

"*Chief* Harper," he said.

"I know who you are," Cori said. "And you know what I do. But we're both off duty tonight, right?"

"Absolutely," he said. "So I only have one question for you."

She offered a bring-it-on smirk. "Shoot."

"Do you take those gloves off to eat your free fries?"

"Please," she said, turning to go. "That's what forks are for, Chief."

"I'M NOT sure I like your new friends," he said as he pulled in beside my barn.

"I know. We can't agree on everything, can we?"

"No. We just have to agree on enough."

His comment sounded slightly ominous, so I didn't reply. Besides, I was distracted by the three sets of glowing eyes on the hood of my truck.

Kellan noticed them too as he turned off the lights of his SUV. "What was that?"

"The cats I mentioned earlier. They're keeping an eye on me."

"More like six eyes. It's kind of... eerie."

"Sure is," I said, laughing. "There's something we can agree on."

I thought he'd be unnerved by the audience, but he just shrugged and turned in his seat. "If you're in agreement, I'd like to kiss you goodnight."

"Very much so," I said. "I'm glad you're not worried about the kits in the cheap seats."

"There's that wit. It's one of the things I love about you."

A thrill ran up my spine. "There's more?" I asked, as he leaned in.

"You smell good," he said. "I always think of you when I smell ketchup. Brings back high school."

I let him link his fingers through mine. "That may just be the nicest thing anyone has ever said to me."

"Can we agree to stop talking now?"

I didn't technically agree but I did follow his lead, and the conversation ended far better than I could have imagined.

CHAPTER TWENTY-THREE

K eats didn't need to stare me awake the next morning. I'd hardly slept a wink, but for a change there was an almost equal amount of excitement mixed in with my dread about what the day held. The tension at the inn would no doubt continue until there was solid proof that one of the Bridge Buddies had committed a bigger crime than sweeping a good hand of cards off the table. My money was on Morag, simply because a mother's wrath was likely deeper than a wife scorned. But what did I know? I was neither of those things.

"It shouldn't shock me that all of this happened in Clover Grove," I told Keats as we walked through the wet grass to get to the barn. I could have taken the flagstone path but I enjoyed seeing the double trail we left behind us. Keats and I liked to go our own way most of the time.

He offered what sounded like a disgusted commentary on the sordid affair, but his tail told a different story. After an evening spent helping my mom minister to the nails of the Bridge Buddies, he was excited to be getting on with things.

Today I got wise and looked up even before unlocking the

henhouse. Sure enough, the tricky trio was sitting on the roof in the dawn gloom and staring down into my flashlight's beam.

"Again?" I said. "You don't need fresh chicken for breakfast. Jilly told me you ate six tins of tuna between you last night. And she's poaching you a salmon for breakfast. She says you deserve it more than our guests."

If they were excited or grateful they didn't show it. Several cats had cycled in and out of our family home as I was growing up but none had stayed long enough for me to grow truly accustomed to their ways. Mom claimed to be allergic to pets, when really she was just allergic to more work. I guess with six kids and a string of crappy jobs that was understandable, although I resented her for it at the time. Now I realized I was born a pet-lover and those urges were thwarted and sublimated. Maybe if I'd had the dog I always wanted I wouldn't have ended up so miserable in corporate life.

On the other hand, without that misery, I wouldn't have found Keats, got conked in the head and landed here. So, maybe it was time to cut Mom some slack. No need to go overboard, but I could release some old grudges. Especially after she threw herself into the breach with the Bridge Buddies last night. I knew that was her way of apologizing for what she'd said at the family meeting, so I'd forgive her for that, too.

"I learned to speak dog pretty fast," I said now, to the dog who taught me. "I guess I could learn cat, too."

Unlocking the henhouse, I flashed the light at the trio again. "You can't come in. My chickens are strictly off limits. But I will do my very best to understand what you're trying to tell me about Ed—"

Panther let out a growling yodel that drowned out the word.

"About your former benefactor," I said. "But you need to respect the sanctity of my henhouse."

Keats growled too, but as he stared up at them with his blue eye, the sound died in this throat.

"Take it easy on my dog, too," I said. "He's got a job to do. I need him at the top of his game—not freaking out because you're ambushing him."

Keats wagged an enthusiastic endorsement.

"Otherwise, you are welcome to be cats of leisure. I'm fine with giving you a free ride here, although I wouldn't say no if you decided to evict the vermin." I pulled open the henhouse door. "I don't really want to know about your strategies, though. I try to run a humane operation here."

The cats didn't move as I went inside with Keats and switched on the lights. Aladdin jumped off his perch with a big commotion, as if embarrassed to be caught asleep on the job.

"It's okay, handsome," I said. "You've got a few minutes to get your game face on. I beat the dawn again."

I walked out into their fenced pen to make sure there were no tears in the heavy gauge double screening. It would take a real panther—or a human with tools—to gain access, but it paid to check. Everything looked in good order, but the cats had come to crouch on top of the outdoor pen.

"Off," I said, flicking my hand with the light. "Chickens may not be rocket scientists but they know a triple threat when they see one. And guess what happens with stressed hens? No omelettes for hungry guests. The hens' happiness is paramount. You've got the run of the entire farm, so go have fun."

They disappeared from view and I watched their silhouettes against the sunrise as they raced off on official cat business.

Keats practically heaved a sigh of relief beside me. His tail fanned happily as he escorted Aladdin out first to greet the day. As the rooster did his thing, I walked among the rows of nest boxes, gently rousing the ladies. They rose, one by one, fluttering sleepily and making the peeping noises of contented fowl. I was coming to know some of the vocal cues of my animals and they were a helpful shortcut in figuring out how to meet their needs.

I collected the eggs, grateful for the ritual that forced me to stay present, at least for half an hour. Keats escorted them out to the yard, but Sookie was in no hurry. Of all the hens, she was the most determined to stay put and hatch that egg. I hated to do it, but some days I had to pick her up and transport her outside by hand.

"One day, Sookie," I said. "Next spring you can raise some chicks. I promise."

Her clucks turned into a flapping protest and for the first time she tried to give me a savage peck.

"None of that, lady." I set her down quickly outside. "Keats, take the protective mama to Aladdin so that she can fall in love all over."

He did that while I collected the feed and refreshed the water. Soon the flock was getting on with their day, leaving Keats and me to get on with ours.

After the rest of our chores, I said, "Into the truck, buddy. There's something I need to put behind me and today's the day. Otherwise I may spend it mooning over Kellan, when there's still a murder to solve."

The truck stalled twice during the drive, and I wasn't too surprised. I was nervous, no question about that. Flashbacks of my run-in with Lloyd Boyce's killer escaped from wherever they were normally stored and raced around my mind unleashed. That was the main problem with driving stick, I decided. You had to focus so much on the task that it left the mental fortress unattended. Too long and I was seriously undermined.

Keats rested his white paw on mine as I shifted gears, and that steadied me. Normally he'd be up on the dash trying to steer but as always, he knew when I needed an extra injection of his special magic.

As we approached the country store, I saw that the old sign I'd known all my life had been replaced. The new one looked quaint without tipping over into kitsch. Where it had once read "Myrtle's Country Store," today it said, "Mandy's Country Café."

Mandy McCain opened the doors at seven but she was normally there by five to start baking. When the breeze was right, I could smell her sweet work from the farm.

The coffee smelled even better as I walked inside with Keats. In the past month, Mandy had been gradually having the place renovated. The grocery rows had been cut back to make room for half a dozen round café tables that supplemented the coveted row of stools at the window.

A pretty, old-fashioned glass case sat beside the cash register, holding pedestal dishes with layer cakes, several pies, and platters of Mandy's popular squares.

"Morning, Ivy," she said, as she arranged apple oat bars on a tray. In harvest time, apples were the region's dominant theme, followed closely by pumpkin. "Apple bar with your coffee?"

"Yeah," I said. "Breakfast of champions."

Her eyes didn't quite meet mine and I knew she was as unnerved as I was about what had happened with her grandmother, Myrtle. It wasn't Mandy's fault and I knew that, but she hadn't been fully forthcoming, and withholding information had nearly gotten me killed. Still, I understood the extenuating circumstances and was determined to put this tension between us to rest. I'd always loved this store, and with the changes she was making, I could love it again. For the past month I'd mostly had baked goods delivered so that I could avoid going in. Worse, I'd been letting Jilly do more of the baking, which was work she didn't need. It didn't make sense when desserts were Mandy's gift.

"I'll have it here," I said. "With a large coffee, please."

Mandy's hand shook a little as she set a mug on the counter. She had been painfully shy in our school days, and while that was easing now, she was never going to be a social butterfly.

There was no one else in the store, so when she delivered the warm oat square, I invited her to join me. Keats sat like a statue beside me, exuding disapproval. He wasn't giving up a grudge that easily.

Mandy perched on the edge of a hoop backed chair, ready to take flight at the first sign of tension.

"Mandy, I—"

"Ivy, I—"

Our voices overlapped and we both laughed. I raised my hand to go first. "All I want to say is, 'water under the bridge.' We're both good people and I hope we can be good neighbors and friends during a long life here in Clover Grove."

We could be part of a new age of true community as the Bridge Buddies and their ilk eventually moved on to greener pastures.

Tears filled Mandy's blue eyes and spilled down her pale cheeks. "I'm so happy to hear you say that. I've felt terrible over what happened and didn't know what to do. You know how awkward I am."

I reached out and patted her hand that sat on the table. "What I know is that you're making this place yours with grace and confidence. You should be proud of yourself."

"I'm trying," she said, pulling the tie out of her fine, dirty blonde hair and shaking it loose. "It's been tough. A lot of people boycott the place because of what happened, but I'm counting on the smell of baked goods to draw them back in."

"It worked on me," I said, smiling. "Your hair looks amazing, by the way. You've had a makeover."

"Robbi convinced me that good hair was half the battle," she said.

"That salon's a theater of war," I said, slicing into the oat bar with my fork. "I'm impressed you went in."

"Oh, I didn't. Her regulars terrify me. Gertrude and Morag in particular."

"I hear you. They're still at the inn, and less susceptible to baked goods than most guests."

She laughed. "I know. I'm glad they don't come in here often."

"Were any of them here the day before Edna's death?" I was a little surprised at how easily that lie tripped off my tongue. I'd been a master of evasion in HR but outright lying was a newer skill.

Mandy leaned back and crossed her thin arms. If she consumed any of her baked goods, she burned off the calories with nervous energy. "All of them, actually. Gertrude, Morag, Joan and Annamae came for coffee in the morning. They stayed for a good hour and it sounded like they were having a strategy session."

"Strategy? What kind of strategy?"

"Bridge strategy. It was all about cards and tricks and terminology I didn't know. They stopped talking when I came around with refills." She frowned. "That's when they took a few jabs at my hair. I'd had it done the day before and it had gone flat, I guess. They always find something, don't they?"

"They make fun of me, too," I assured her. "Do you mind if I ask about the status of the crème brûlée at that point? Did any of them have access to it?"

"Probably. Like I already told Chief Harper, it was a busy day. When I'm at the cash register, anyone could slip into the kitchen. No one wants to work for me so I'm on my own right now."

"And you baked the custard that morning?"

She shook her head. "At home, the night before. Crème brûlée is best chilled overnight."

Sipping my coffee, I pondered. "Well, I'm no further ahead. All of those women had access."

"Edna, too. She was in that afternoon and ate two slices of chocolate cake. Normally she's too frugal for that."

"Nervous, probably," I said. "This was after her perm?"

Mandy's fine eyebrows rose. "If she'd had a perm it didn't take too well. It was a windy day and when she took off her wool hat the static did a number on it. I remember thinking the Bridge Buddies would razz her for that, like they did mine. But I passed her outside Robbi's later so she probably fixed it for her. I hope it looks nice for the funeral," she finished, looking a little guilty.

"Poor Edna. The Bridge Buddies really had it out for her." I tried to wash down the oat bar with too much coffee and choked a little.

"There were so many secrets," Mandy said. "My grand—I mean Myrtle—used to tell me about their scandals. I suppose it caused tension that Edna had dirt on them from her job." She pushed back the chair and rose. "Chief Harper has his work cut out for him, that's for sure."

I gave up on the square and rubbed my face with both hands. "It feels like this will never get solved and my inn will never be cleared."

Mandy looked down at me and color filled her pale cheeks. "I bet it felt that way with Lloyd Boyce at one point, too."

"Yeah," I said. I found myself smiling and it wasn't even forced. "You're right about that."

After collecting the box of desserts for the inn, I walked out to the truck with Keats. "Comfort comes from the strangest places sometimes, buddy. It really pays to keep an open mind."

CHAPTER TWENTY-FOUR

"What should we do now?" I asked Keats as I turned the key in the ignition. "Try Merle's granddaughter, maybe? Or Morag's daughter?" I glanced at him. "That would be a touchy one. And I'm steering far clear of the Bridge Buddy men. My nosiness only goes so far."

Keats normally had his tail up, ready for the next quest, but now he sat down, wrapping the white tuft neatly around white paws. He stared at me with his blue eye, and I sensed I was barking up the wrong tree.

"Okay, your tail says wrong trail. Would you care to be more explicit before I start driving? Should I go into town and poke around?"

He stayed as he was, a black-and-white statue with an eerie eye. Then he tilted his head and mumbled something that was more than a suggestion.

"You want to go home? Already? Are you okay?"

His mouth fell open in an easy smile. He was fine. He put his paws on the dash to confirm it.

"Is something wrong on the farm?" I pressed. "You never pass up the opportunity to nose around for clues."

He mumbled something else and I gave in. "Fine. Have it your way. I suppose I'm just trying to avoid my own home, anyway. I cannot stand those women." I pulled out of Mandy's parking lot and headed toward home. Keats looked relieved, but his tail didn't come up as I'd expected. Something was definitely off with him today. Maybe leaving the cats unsupervised was worrying him. I could hardly blame him for that. They were an unpredictable lot.

"I'm missing something, Keats," I said, gearing up with a couple of significant bunny hops. "I sense it. Can you?"

Without turning, he offered three quick pants: yes-yes-yes.

"If you know what, it wouldn't hurt to drop a clue." He mumbled something that sounded like, "I already have, stupid."

Laughing, I turned into the long lane and drove slowly under the "Runaway Farm" sign with its permanently missing "m." I'd runaway far from Clover Grove and then run back here to stay. I loved that constant reminder of my journey. Especially when I wanted to run again.

Fleecy, the white cat, was sitting in the middle of the lane just as it opened to the parking area. She turned and dashed off toward the henhouse, making Keats growl.

"Was that cat standing guard?" I said. "They're up to something, I know it."

Keats grumbled an affirmative, and he didn't wait politely to be released from the truck. Instead, he charged right over me as I opened the door, and raced after Fleecy.

"Thanks," I said, rubbing my legs. Now I was going to have to break up a fight. I hoped no one lost an eye, including me.

A cacophony started up with loud barking and even louder yowling from the cats. What was it about cat wailing that made it so spooky, even in broad daylight? The hair on my arms and the back of my neck rose.

"Honestly," I said, going behind the barn. "Is this drama really necessary? Time to work it out, kids."

But when I saw what was really going on, I screamed, too. "Get off there right now!"

The three cats had completely shredded the screen on the window over the door where Edna had broken in the other day. Panther was literally clinging with one paw and clawing away at it with the other. As I watched, he hoisted himself easily over the edge and disappeared inside. Fleecy went next but Big Red sat on the roof, waiting for me to do something.

Keats stood on his hind legs like a circus dog, barking his throat raw. There was nothing he could do, and he wasn't used to being helpless when his charges were under attack. I felt his frustration in my chest and that soon turned to fury. How dare they take advantage of my kindness like that? They were well fed and had no reason at all to pick easy marks like my hens. Cats would be cats, but there were plenty of challenges with the rodents inside the barn.

I ran around to Wilma's pen to get the pig poker. I didn't want to hurt them but I wouldn't hesitate to take a few jabs if they were mangling my chickens. I took a quick look into the chicken yard as I passed and saw their little door was still open, meaning some of them could be inside. Trapped.

My hands trembled as I fumbled for the right key to unlock the door. I tripped on the doorstep and almost fell as I entered. Flipping on the light, I looked around. There were only four hens inside and all of them were sitting, quite calmly, on nest boxes. One of them was Sookie. That broody hen was trying to force out a second egg. She was determined to be a mom.

"Where are you?" I demanded. "Show yourselves, cats."

Keats, of course, pointed them out for me. All three had positioned themselves on the shelf directly above Sookie. The hen looked around with bright eyes. I couldn't tell if she sensed the threat, but she wasn't making a move to leave.

Brandishing the pig poker, I said, "Back away slowly and go out the way you came in. No one needs to get hurt."

The cats didn't move. I mean, they literally didn't flick a whisker. They could have been taxidermies, except for the fact that blood trickled off the shelf in front of Panther and splashed Sookie's box on the way down. He'd broken a claw or two during the break-in.

"I'm sorry you're hurt, but that serves you right," I said, staring at him. He stared back, unblinking. Never had I seen such a defiant animal, and that included an irascible sow.

I gave the shelf they were sitting on a good thwack. It was enough to rattle my teeth, but it didn't make the cats flinch. Sookie, however, got flustered. She flapped her wings and let out a squawk.

The cats now stood as one and I had to make a tough decision. Swipe at them with the poker or put it down and grab the bird? I'd need both hands for the latter.

"Get the other three hens outside," I said to Keats, and he turned quickly. They were on the lowest shelf and easily prodded out of their boxes and through the side door.

Meanwhile, I rested the poker in the corner without turning my back for a second, and then reached slowly for Sookie. If she took flight, the cats would be on her in a second.

I heaved a sigh of relief when I got the hen in my hands and pressed her gently to my chest. The poor sweet bird Edna loved had nearly become a clucking canapé for the woman's own cats. If this was how they thanked their patron, they were unwelcome at Runaway Farm. Charlie had some live traps and I would get them set up today and export these ingrates to Cori or Bridget. Let the feisty felines try their luck in Dog Town.

When Keats came back in, I released Sookie into the yard and shut the little escape hatch. We'd have to repair the window today and figure out a way to secure it while still providing the ventilation the birds needed.

I turned back, expecting the cats to be gone. Instead, they'd come down from the shelf. Panther had squished himself onto the nest box and stared at me now from close range. If I hadn't seen with my own eyes that there was no egg, I'd swear he was trying to hatch one. Red and Fleecy flanked him, fixing their big eyes on me.

"What is with you guys?" I said.

Panther's paw hung over the side of the box and blood dribbled down and into the cracks of Sookie's designer digs.

The anger drained out of me instantly as I realized they hadn't been trying to kill Sookie after all. They were more interested in her roost.

"Okay, off," I said more gently. "Let me take a look at this and see what's worth clawing yourself bloody over."

Panther immediately vacated, and I examined the nest box closely. It was different from the others, taller and deeper, because Edna had insisted Sookie would only lay if she had the height advantage over the other hens. I wasn't familiar enough with chickens to say one way or the other, but Sookie laid reliably so I figured Edna knew her hen best. Now I wondered if there was more to the story than that.

Prying the nest box loose, I turned it over. Ah! A false bottom. I pulled away the small, sliding board and found a metal lockbox.

"What the heck? Is that why Agatha was creeping around here that morning? Did she know Edna had stashed something in here?"

I glanced up at the cats and three sets of eyes blinked what felt like an affirmative.

"How do I... Oh! The key from the doll's head," I said. Keats, who'd pretty much stayed silent till now, mumbled encouragement. It was his find, after all.

Pulling my key ring out of my front pocket, I flipped through them before I found the tiny one buried by the others. Sure enough, it fit neatly into the lock. Setting the metal box on the shelf below Sookie's spot, I turned on my phone light and lifted the lid.

Inside was a ring box, among other jewels, and all sat atop a small stack of yellowed letters. Now I knew why Edna had said this was personal. There was no doubt in my mind that this box represented the broken heart she'd shut down and stowed away.

I felt terrible opening the ring box, but I needed to confirm my suspicions. Sure enough, when I flipped the lid there was a ring with a diamond larger than I'd ever seen. It sat in a vintage style platinum setting and glinted gorgeously under my flashlight.

"Wowza! No wonder Merle's family wants that back."

I couldn't resist trying it on my left ring finger and angling it to see the different facets. Rainbows bounced off the homely henhouse walls.

Glancing from Keats to the cats, I said, "What? A woman can dream, right?"

Aiming the light into the metal box, I inspected the rest of the contents. There was a sapphire-encrusted broach, an emerald pendant and another ring with a smaller diamond. These, I assumed, were Edna's family jewels.

"Okay, cat army, you can stand down," I said. "We'll lock these back up and take them someplace safe."

I expected a mumble of endorsement from Keats. Instead, there was a chilling growl in his throat. His ruff had come up and his tail stood out stiff and straight, as it only did in times of terrible trouble. Unfortunately, I had reason to know.

The cats arched, one-two-three, and their hissing almost drowned out the voice softly calling my name.

CHAPTER TWENTY-FIVE

I knew that voice. It was familiar but completely out of context and I couldn't place it.

Regardless, my companions were quite clear that it was time to take evasive maneuvers. First I latched the door from the inside as gently and quietly as I could. Then I closed the lid of the metal box and shoved it behind a sack of wood shavings.

"Who's there?" I called, pulling out my phone and texting Jilly quickly: *Henhouse 911*.

There was a gentle knock at the door. "Just me."

It still wasn't enough for me to place her. I signaled Keats to be quiet and the cats followed the order, too.

"I'm in the middle of something," I called. "Who's there?"

"It's a surprise." The woman's voice was soft. Beguiling. Utterly false. If I had real hackles, they'd knock my head off.

"Can't," I called. "I'm cleaning the coop. Give me 10 minutes and we'll meet on the porch."

"Okay."

Again the voice was sweet and calm. I heaved a sigh. Ten minutes was plenty of time for Jilly to do something. I texted Kellan for good measure.

I blocked the door as well as I could with the pig poker, thinking hard. The voice hadn't belonged to one of the Bridge Buddies, I was quite sure of that. Could it be Kimberly or Stacy, their game partners? I hadn't spent enough time chatting with them to be sure.

But I'd definitely heard this voice before and Keats thought so, too.

As I added a shovel and rake to the barricade, my unconscious mind worked overtime. One by one pieces started to drop into place. Finally, I remembered what I had seen and overlooked at Edna's. I connected it with threads of conversations I'd heard from the Bridge Buddies and what I heard from Mandy that morning.

Now I knew who it was. And obviously I knew what she wanted: Edna's magic bird box. But even with the big ring glinting off my left hand, I didn't see how this was worth killing for.

If I hadn't been rattling tools around and mulling, I probably would have heeded Keats' repeated whines and looked up. I may have had time to arm myself before the intruder poked her head into the upper window.

Gorgeous highlighted hair draped over the ledge for just a second as she climbed in swiftly and jumped.

She took me down hard enough to knock the breath right out of me and then knelt on my chest to make sure it didn't come back.

"You really need to stop sticking your head into dangerous holes, Ivy," Robbi Ford said. "It's a total waste of a beautiful haircut."

I tried to squirm out from under her but she had 30 pounds on me, and the upper hand. Then I considered my signature head butt, the one that worked on Lloyd's attacker, but she seemed to anticipate that and leaned just far enough back.

Where was Keats? Why wasn't he doing his thing?

It wasn't long—but it felt like hours—before it became clear that the cats and dog had devised a plan. Or at least different plans that dovetailed perfectly. The cats flitted to the top shelf and their butts waggled as they waited for the perfect moment to pounce. Meanwhile there was crazed squawking outside, which quickly changed to crazed squawking *inside*. Keats had brought 40 birds back in to flutter and flap in seeming pandemonium. Robbi let go of me to swat them away from her head, and that's when the cats launched in unison. Big Red was in the middle like a bolt of feline lightning. He landed on Robbi's head and spun like a dervish, clawing her scalp until her hair flew off in clumps. I screamed in horror, too, before realizing it was actually hair extensions. Those gorgeous locks were as fake as she was.

She rolled off me and curled up on the floor, shielding her head with her arms. Keats circled her, growling as I'd never heard him before. He was looking for a way in, to seize and lacerate her ear, but she offered no purchase.

Meanwhile I turned swiftly and grabbed the pig poker. It had stood me in good stead many times, but it would be tricky to use it with so many animals stalking, leaping, and fluttering. In small confines, it was complete chaos.

In the end I settled for pressing the hook against her midriff. It wouldn't do as much damage but it would slow her down enough that Keats could get at her if she unfurled. The security squad seemed to understand I had the matter in hand and settled down.

"Why, Robbi?" I asked. Simple. Easy. Terribly complex.

"It was supposed to be Edna," she said. "Aggie and I had it all arranged. We'd kill her together and split the proceeds. But Aggie kept dragging her heels. She couldn't or wouldn't get the job done. So I told her to stand down and let me take care of it."

"You were there. At Edna's house," I said. "I saw the scissors."

"I did a home visit two weeks ago. Collected the poison from her old medical kit, just like Aggie told me. I was going to slip it to her when I did her perm, but this was easier."

"Because you could frame the Bridge Buddies."

"All of them are capable," she said. "Trust me."

"But none of them need the money like you and Aggie."

"My shop is going under and it's the bridge club's fault. They're scaring customers away with their foolishness. They're like a gang, and Edna was part of that. When Aggie showed up in town and told me about the ring and family jewels that were rightfully hers anyway, we decided to team up. At the last minute Aggie got cold feet and took off."

"She got cold feet alright," I said. "You killed the wrong twin."

The remains of her hair flipped as she uncovered her head to stare at me. "*What?*"

"Aggie ate the crème brûlée and died a perm-free death."

"That stupid, greedy sow." Her eyes shut for a second, and then popped open, glinting evilly in a dusty beam of light from the window overhead. "Then Edna's alive. To die again."

She unfurled suddenly, knocked the pole aside and kicked my feet out from under me. Where a hairdresser learned moves like that I didn't know.

Grabbing the poker, she pressed it to my forehead. "I'll find Edna and finish my business. She owes me. Now... give me the jewelry. Aggie swore it was in here. I've had a heck of a time getting in, between your cameras and the stupid cats dive-bombing me. When I saw you hugging it out with Mandy this morning, I knew you were putting the pieces together. It was now or never."

I gestured to the bag of wood shavings. "The box is under there."

She turned to grab it and I rolled, grabbed the shovel, and jumped to my feet. When she turned back, holding the box, we were both armed.

"I'll kill your dog if you move," she said. "Nothing would give me more pleasure." She managed to open the unlocked box while still brandishing the poker. Then she gave a guttural scream of pure rage. "Where is it? The big diamond ring is missing."

"I don't know," I said. "Really I don't."

"Hold out your hands right now."

I did as I was told, and she stared at my bare hands.

That brief pause gave Keats his chance to turn into a canine rocket. As always, he nailed his mark. The cats launched again from the shelf a second later. Then the hens whirled up in feathered outrage.

Robbi went down once more, shrieking, and the old love letters flew about the coop, buffeted by wings.

The door opened abruptly and Kellan appeared, larger than life and never so welcome. Within seconds his officers restrained Robbi, and he turned to me.

"Stand down, Ivy," he said. "I've got this."

Only then did I realize I was still poised to take someone out with the shovel. He had to unfurl my fingers from the handle one by one and remove it with a tug.

He tried to catch me as I dropped to the floor but I wasn't collapsing, just reaching for Keats. After a few minutes of hugging my dog and whispering sweet nothings in his ear, I peered around. "We've got to find that ring, Kellan," I said. "It means everything to Edna and Merle."

CHAPTER TWENTY-SIX

Later, after the Bridge Buddies had scattered for their homes, Jilly and I took Keats for a walk in the meadows. The grass was brown and brittle but the trees were still bright. The color was definitely hanging on longer than usual this year.

"What a relief to see the end of that crew," Jilly said, pulling a baseball cap over her golden curls. "I bet those ringers will never come near Clover Grove again."

She looked tired and frazzled, and I knew I looked far worse. I hadn't even bothered to shower or change yet, and my jacket was liberally sprinkled with chicken poop and feathers. Turns out, a big flock of scared birds could eject a whole lot of guano.

"I'm pretty sure the Bridge Buddies won't be able to sucker anyone into backing them, no matter how much money they offer." I looked over at Jilly. "Do you think they'll badmouth the inn?"

"Are you kidding? With the dirt we have on them, they'll be as sweet as apple pie to us for the rest of their days." She grinned at me. "At least to our faces."

"In other words, we've become Edna Evans," I said. "Keeper of secrets."

She scrunched her pretty face. "We're nothing like Edna, no

matter how much she's redeemed herself. She's not going to turn into a sweet little old lady because of this."

"Agreed," I said. "It's baked into the bone, now. But she's softening a little. When I spoke to her on the phone, I asked her to give the ring to Merle's granddaughter, in case she changes her mind about wanting to wear the family ring. Edna didn't say no."

"The ring that's missing in action?" Jilly said.

"It'll turn up," I said. "The police are pretty much tearing the coop apart right now to find it. I couldn't stand to watch. The poor hens are in an uproar and Charlie's moving them out."

"How did you finally put the pieces together about Robbi?" Jilly asked.

"Mandy's hair," I said. "I realized Robbi had done a home visit on the night Mandy made the crème brûlée. Plus, I'd seen Robbi's fancy shears at Edna's place when we broke in, so I knew she could have picked up the poison then." I kicked at the grass. "I just wish I'd figured it out earlier. She saw me with Mandy and followed me home."

"Better late than never," Jilly said. "Who spiked Edna's driveway with nails?"

"That was Aggie. Kellan thinks she was trying to scare me away from Edna. She was worried we were getting close and I guess she was right."

"What do you mean?"

"Among the love letters was Edna's new will. She'd named me as her beneficiary."

Jilly gasped, and then beamed. "So you really were getting through to her."

"More likely she wanted to stop Aggie from getting any more of her worldly goods."

"Or she felt guilty about what happened with Lloyd," Jilly suggested.

I shrugged. "Either way, I doubt she'll be vying for best friend status. It's still Edna. But maybe we'll see more glimmers of her good side when she gets home."

"No sugar, no pie," Jilly said, and we both laughed.

After tossing a stick for Keats, I burst out laughing again. "Kellan's uniform is a disaster. He'll probably throw another one out and start fresh."

"Dating you could get expensive," she said.

"That reminds me... I'll need to replace your second favorite sweater. There was an incident at the restaurant."

Jilly just laughed. "I'm willing to sacrifice a sweater for the cause. Should we invite the guys for leftover pizza tonight?"

"Sure, if we're awake that long." I noticed a path into the woods to our right. "That one leads to Edna's house. Do you mind if we make a pit stop?"

When we got there, two dozen cats scattered from Edna's front porch like leaves in the wind. Panther, Fleecy and Big Red held their ground.

"Ah, I see," Jilly said. "You're checking on the war heroes."

Keats made a big show of storming around with his tail high but he lacked his usual verve. The big three could tell he was bluffing and didn't bother moving.

"Hey guys," I said, stopping at the bottom of the stairs. "Just wanted to say thanks. You really had my back and I appreciated it. Keats did, too, although he won't admit it."

They stared at me and then blinked as one. How'd they do that?

"So let me get this right," Jilly said. "You're a cat whisperer now, too."

"Far from it. I don't even have my learner's permit for cat. Seems like there's no end of languages to learn if you want to be a successful hobby farmer. And country sleuth."

"If anyone can do it, you can," Jilly said. "You're the brightest person I know. With the brightest dog I know." She looked up at the porch. "And now the brightest cats, too."

"The cats are Edna's," I said. "Although maybe my old barn cats will reconsider now that Keats is simmering down."

We went around the back of the house and topped up the food and water at the new feeding station I'd set up on the porch, in hopes of luring the cats out of the swamp for easier capture .

"Enjoy your victory feast," I called, as we headed down the front drive. "Thanks again."

We walked in companionable silence till we were almost home and then Jilly said, "You should call your mom and tell her what happened."

I rolled my eyes. "Did you have to go and ruin a perfect moment by bringing up my mom?"

"She came through for you last night, remember? Those ladies were purring like kittens after your mom and Iris spoiled them." She pondered for a second. "They're quite talented, you know. Maybe they should take over Robbi's salon."

I closed my eyes and Keats gently nudged me away from a deep pothole. "That's a recipe for trouble, Jilly. Mom can't hold down a job and they'll end up embroiled in town politics."

"Just a thought," she said. "Do I need to point out that I have a good head for career development?"

"No, but I'd prefer you help me develop some new guests for the inn. Nice ones next time."

"We'll brainstorm," she said. "Tomorrow. For now, how about showers, lunch, a nap and a hot double date... in exactly that order?"

"Heaven," I said. "Keats, I have bad news. I'm not the only one who needs a shower. You stink of chicken poop and maybe a little nervous cat pee."

He glared up at me with the full force of his blue eye.

"And now more bad news for Keats," Jilly said, as we started up the front stairs of the inn.

Lounging comfortably on the porch swing was Big Red, the marmalade cat. He looked very much at home and I suspected he intended to make that arrangement permanent.

"Uh-oh," I said. "I foresee future turf wars."

"Make that present," Jilly said, as Keats charged and Red arched and hissed.

"Boys, enough," I said. "Jilly and I have earned some downtime. You can pick up where you left off later."

I opened the front door and both animals proceeded inside, jockeying for position in the doorway. The cat was ahead by a whisker and Keats whined pathetically.

Jilly and I looked at each other and laughed again.

"BEAUTIFUL NIGHT," Kellan said, wrapping his arm around my shoulders as we stared up at the moon from the backyard. "But it was even nicer by the fire. Wasn't it?"

"Nature needs to take its course," I said, as Keats nosed around the lawn, seemingly in no hurry to do his business.

"You fed that dog a fair bit of steamed broccoli. Do you think that was wise?" Kellan asked.

"I do," I said. "I think it was wise indeed."

"The air was a little ripe in the family room. That's all I'm saying." He shrugged. "I guess you know what's best for a dog's innards."

I looked up at Big Red, who was sitting above us on the back deck. "You could hurry things along if you tried," I said.

The cat gave an elaborate yawn and then flitted down the stairs. He tiptoed across the wet grass and then, when he was just a few feet behind Keats, arched his back and spit.

Keats leapt into the air and took off, and the cat chased him. Suddenly Keats remembered his heritage and turned back, circling and looping. Every time he got within range the cat would take a crazy leap in another direction.

"That was a little mean," Kellan said, shaking his head over their antics. "Doesn't Keats deserve a quiet night after his heroics this morning?"

"Now he can have it because nature is taking its course. He's motion activated, you see." I pulled a couple of poop bags out of my pocket and walked over to the dog. "Can you shine your light right here?"

"Me? What? No! It's disgusting."

"Kellan! Who's the fearsome chief of police now?"

"I've suffered enough poop today." But he held his breath and did as I asked. "What on earth is that?"

I stooped and scooped very carefully. "That, my friend, is a three-carat antique diamond ring. In the middle of the scuffle with Robbi, I felt Keats snatch it off my ring finger. Later I realized he must have swallowed the evidence to keep it safe. I've been waiting all day to be proven right."

Kellan shook his head, clearly impressed. Revolted, yet impressed. "That dog continues to surprise me."

"Me too," I said. "Would you like to deliver this treasure to Edna and surprise her?"

He gasped for air. "You can do the honors. May I suggest you restore it to its original sparkle first? Edna may not be able to handle that."

"I firmly believe that woman could survive anything," I said. "But yeah, I'll buff it up nicely and then drive her over to give it to her old beau's granddaughter. The bride need never know where it's been."

He walked me back to the house, keeping more of a distance. "So you tried the ring on, did you?"

My face heated up and I was grateful for the darkness. "Just for a second. It was way too fancy for a farmer, that's for sure."

"I don't know about that," Kellan said, opening the door with a slight bow. "You and your prize mutt here deserve nothing but the finest."

As we all settled again by the hearth, I looked around and then shook my head in disbelief. Jilly had certainly been right about the complexities of our new life, but now, with one hand in Kellan's and the other touching Keats' soft ears, my heart filled with a deep contentment I'd never truly known before. In this moment, surrounded by my nearest and dearest, life felt delightfully simple.

Please sign up for my mailing list to find out more about this series and my work. My newsletter is full of funny stories and photos of my adorable dogs. Don't miss out!

RUNAWAY FARM & INN RECIPES

Mandy's Frozen Lemon Dazzle Cake

Ingredients

2 packages of ladyfinger cookies
5 eggs, separated
¾ cup freshly squeezed lemon juice
1 ¼ cup of sugar
Rind of one lemon, grated finely
2 cups of whipping cream
4 tbsp icing sugar
Dash of cream of tartar

Directions

Butter a 10-inch springform pan. Line bottom and sides with ladyfinger cookies.

In a heavy saucepan, beat 5 egg yolks and 2 eggs whites until thick (keeping whites of three eggs aside). Add lemon juice, rind and sugar. Cook over low heat until thickened.

Cool lemon mixture completely. Whip the heavy cream and then fold into the lemon curd. Pour into the prepared pan. Cover tightly and freeze at least six hours, preferably overnight.

The next day, beat the remaining three egg whites with icing sugar and cream of tartar until stiff peaks form. Spread over frozen torte.

Place under the broiler and watch like a hawk until slightly browned. Cool for a few minutes, and then return to freezer until ready to serve. Defrost at least an hour before serving.

Serves 10-12.

Made in United States
North Haven, CT
25 February 2023